The Three Investigators in

The Mystery of
the Silver Spider

ALFRED HITCHCOCK

and The Three Investigators in

The Mystery
of the
Silver
Spider

Text by Robert Arthur
Illustrated by Harry Kane

RANDOM HOUSE · NEW YORK

CONTENTS

A SHORT PREVIEW
BY ALFRED HITCHCOCK

"We Investigate Anything" is the motto of The Three Investigators—Jupiter Jones, Pete Crenshaw and Bob Andrews, all from Rocky Beach, California, near the fabulous city of Hollywood. And so they do, as those of you who have made their acquaintance in earlier books well know.

This time they leave their snug Headquarters in the super-junkyard known as The Jones Salvage Yard to travel overseas and tangle with a sinister plot involving a beautiful silver spider.

I could whet your appetite for adventure by hinting at some of the strange episodes to come, but I shall refrain. All I will say is that as junior secret agents they find themselves mixed up in a plot far bigger and more dangerous than anyone suspected, and before things have quieted down, they—

But there I go! I shall say no more, except to tell you, in case you are meeting them for the first time, that Jupiter Jones, the head of the firm of

The Three Investigators, is known for his remark-
able brain power. Pete Crenshaw is tall and muscu-
lar and excels at athletics. Bob Andrews, the
smallest of the three, attends to research and keeps
records for the firm, but has the courage of a lion
when danger threatens.

And now lights, camera, action! On with the
show!

ALFRED HITCHCOCK

Chapter 1
A Near Miss

"LOOK OUT!" Bob Andrews cried.

"Watch it, Worthington!" echoed Pete Crenshaw.

Worthington, at the wheel of the big, gold-plated Rolls-Royce sedan, jammed on the brakes and The Three Investigators tumbled into a heap in the rear of the car. The Rolls-Royce screamed to a stop scarcely an inch from the side of a gleaming, low-slung limousine.

Instantly several men swarmed out of the limousine. As Worthington descended from the driver's seat, they surrounded him, jabbering excitedly in some strange language. Worthington ignored them. He approached the other car and spoke sternly to the chauffeur, resplendent in a red uniform with gold braid.

"My man," Worthington said, "you ignored a Stop sign. You almost wrecked us both. It was clearly your fault, for I had the right of way."

"Prince Djaro always has the right of way," the other chauffeur answered loftily. He pronounced the name Jar-o. "Others must not get in his way."

By now Pete, Bob and Jupiter had picked themselves up and were looking with amazement at the scene. The men who had popped out of the limousine seemed to be dancing around the tall figure of Worthington in their excitement. One, who was taller than the others and seemed to be in authority, spoke in English.

"Imbecile!" he shouted at Worthington. "You almost killed Prince Djaro! You could have caused an international complication! You should be disciplined."

"I was obeying the traffic laws and you were not," Worthington said stoutly. "Your driver is at fault."

"What's all this about a prince?" Pete muttered to Bob as they watched.

"Don't you read the papers?" Bob whispered back. "He's from Europe—a country called Varania, one of the seven smallest countries in the world. He's visiting the United States on a sightseeing tour."

"Golly! And we almost smashed him into a pretzel!" Pete said.

"Worthington was in the right," Jupiter Jones joined in. "Let's get out and lend him our moral support."

They clambered out of the car. As they did so, the door of the limousine opened and a boy somewhat taller than Bob, with very black hair cut long in European style, stepped down. Though only a couple of years older than the boys, he immediately took charge.

"Silence!" he said, and immediately all of the jabbering men surrounding Worthington became as quiet as clams. He gestured with his hand, and they fell in respectfully behind him as he approached Worthington.

"I should like to apologize," he said, in excellent English. "My driver was at fault. I shall see that he obeys all traffic laws in the future."

"But Your Highness—" protested the tallest man of the group. Prince Djaro waved him to silence. He looked with interest at Bob, Pete and Jupiter as The Three Investigators joined the group.

"I am sorry this happened," he said to them. "Thanks to your chauffeur's skill, a serious accident was prevented. You are the owners of this majestic car?" And he nodded toward the Rolls.

"Not exactly the owners," Jupiter said. "But we use it occasionally." It was hardly the time to go into the history of the Rolls-Royce and the manner in which he had won the use of it in a contest.

As it happened, the three had just been to Hollywood to call on Alfred Hitchcock and give him the facts of their latest adventure. It was in returning home that the near-accident had happened.

"I am Djaro Montestan, of Varania," the boy said. "I'm not really a prince yet, not until I'm officially crowned next month. But I can't keep people from calling me prince. Are you typical American boys?"

It was an odd question. They considered themselves fairly typical American boys but they weren't quite sure what the other boy meant.

Jupiter answered for them.

"Bob and Pete are quite typical of American boys," he said. "I don't suppose you can call me exactly typical because some people think I'm conceited and use too many long words and sometimes get myself pretty well disliked. But I can't seem to change."

Bob and Pete grinned at each other. What Jupiter said was true, though it was the first time they had ever heard him admit it. Because he had a stocky build and was unusually brainy, some people called him a "fat smart alec." But that was just other boys who were envious of him, or adults shown up by his mental ability. His friends swore by him. If they had a problem, they knew Jupiter Jones could solve it if anyone could.

Now Jupe pulled a card from his pocket. It was the official card of The Three Investigators, and he never went anywhere without it.

"Here are our names," he said. "I'm Jupiter Jones, that's Pete Crenshaw, and Bob Andrews."

The foreign boy took the card and read it gravely. It said:

THE THREE INVESTIGATORS
"We Investigate Anything"
? ? ?

First Investigator .... Jupiter Jones
Second Investigator ...... Pete Crenshaw
Records and Research ..... Bob Andrews

They waited, expecting him to ask what the question marks were for. Just about everybody who saw the card asked that.

"Brojas!" Djaro said. He smiled. He had a very nice smile, showing even white teeth against skin a shade darker in complexion than Pete's. "That means 'great' in Varanian. I suppose the question marks are your official symbol."

They looked at him with new respect for having deduced the truth. Djaro took from his own pocket a card which he handed to Jupiter.

"And this," he said, "is my card."

Bob and Pete crowded behind Jupe to look at it. It was very white and very stiff, and in fine engraving said simply *Djaro Montestan*. Above the name was a crest, embossed in gold and blue. It appeared to be a spider on a golden web holding a sword, though it was done so elaborately that it wasn't easy to be sure.

"That is my symbol," the boy said solemnly. "A spider. That is, it is the crest of the reigning family of Varania. It would take too long to tell you how we came to adopt a spider for our national emblem, but I'm very happy to meet you, Pete, Bob, and Jupiter."

And he shook hands with all three of them.

At this point a man pushed his way through to them. He was a slender young man with pleasant, alert features, and he came from a black car that had stopped behind the limousine. As soon as he spoke it was obvious that he was American.

"Excuse me, Your Highness," he said, "but we are

falling behind schedule. I'm happy there wasn't an accident but we ought to be getting on if we're going to tour the city today."

"I'm not especially interested in touring the city," Djaro said. "I've seen a lot of cities. What I want to do is talk to these boys some more. They're the first American boys I've really had a chance to meet.

"Tell me," he added, turning to The Three Investigators, "is Disneyland fun? I've been looking forward to visiting it very much."

They assured him that Disneyland was the greatest, that it shouldn't be missed. Djaro seemed pleased, but wistful.

"It really isn't much fun being surrounded by bodyguards," he said. "Duke Stefan—that's my guardian and the Regent who is running Varania until I am old enough to be crowned prince—apparently gave orders not to let anyone near me for fear I'd catch cold or something. It's ridiculous. I'm not an important head of state whom someone might want to assassinate. Varania has no enemies and I'm really quite unimportant."

He paused a moment, then seemed to make up his mind.

"Will all of you come to Disneyland with me?" he asked. "Show me around and everything? I'd appreciate it very much. I'd like some friends with me for a change."

The request took them by surprise. However, they were perfectly agreeable to a visit to Disneyland, and had nothing else planned for the day. Jupiter made a phone call to his aunt at The Jones Salvage Yard, using the telephone in the Rolls-Royce, while Djaro looked on with great interest. Then the other men squeezed into the U. S. escort car, and Bob, Pete and Jupiter clambered into the limousine with Prince Djaro and the tall, sharp-featured man who had been making such a fuss about the near-accident.

"Duke Stefan will not like this," he said with a dark frown. "He said to take no risks."

"There is no risk, Duke Rojas!" Djaro said curtly. "It is time Duke Stefan learned to like what I like. In two months I will be ruler of my country and my word will be the law, not Duke Stefan's. Now tell Markos to obey all traffic rules henceforth. This is the third time we have almost had a serious accident because he persists in acting as if we were at home in Varania. Let there be no more such happenings!"

Duke Rojas fired off a string of foreign words, and the driver of the car nodded. They got under way again and the boys observed that the driver obeyed all traffic laws after that and drove cautiously.

In the forty-five minutes it took them to get to Disneyland, Prince Djaro was so full of questions about America, and California in particular, that all three were kept busy answering. Then, when they reached Disneyland, they were too busy enjoying themselves on the rides and other attractions to talk much.

At one point, noting that Duke Rojas had lagged behind, Prince Djaro, with a gleam in his eye, suggested they slip away for another trip on the little train that circled the park. Bob, Pete and Jupiter agreed. They ducked quickly behind a crowd of people, then ran up the steps into the miniature station and boarded a train that had just come in. As they rode around the rim of the park, they could see the Duke and his men futilely searching for them below.

When they finally descended, Duke Rojas came running up with several of his men. But before he could open his mouth, Djaro snapped at him, "You did not stay with me. You fell behind. This shall be reported to Duke Stefan."

"But—but—but—" the man sputtered.

Djaro cut him short. "Enough! We go now. I am only sorry my schedule will not let me come back again."

Back at the big car, Djaro ordered Duke Rojas to ride in the following car with the bodyguards. So on the way back to Rocky Beach the four boys could talk freely.

Prince Djaro asked them about themselves, and The Three Investigators took turns telling him how the firm had been started, how they had become friends of Alfred Hitchcock, and of some of the adventures they had had.

"*Brojas!*" the European boy exclaimed. "Oh, but I envy you. American boys have so much freedom. I wish I wasn't a prince—well, I almost wish it. It is my duty to lead my country, small though it is. I have never been to school—I've had tutors all my life—so I have few friends, and I've never done anything exciting until this trip to America. Today is the most fun I've had in all my life.

"May I call you my friends?" he asked. "I'd like to very much."

"We'd be glad to be your friends," Pete said.

"Thank you." Prince Djaro grinned. "Do you know, today is the first time I've ever really talked back to Duke Rojas? It shocked him. It will shock Duke Stefan. They're in for a lot more shocks. After all, I am the prince and I intend to—how do you say it?"

"Assert your authority?" Jupiter suggested, but Bob said, "Throw your weight around."

"That's it, throw my weight around," Djaro said gleefully. "Duke Stefan is in for some surprises."

By now they had reached Rocky Beach. Jupiter gave the driver instructions for finding The Jones Salvage Yard, and in a few moments they pulled through the big iron front gate.

As they got out, Jupiter invited Djaro to see Headquarters. Regretfully, Djaro shook his head.

"I'm afraid there isn't time," he said. "Tonight I have to go to a dinner of some sort, and tomorrow we fly back to Varania. The capital city of Varania is Denzo, and I live there in a palace built on the ruins of an old castle. It has about three hundred rooms, and it is drafty and not too comfortable. That's one of the penalties you have to pay for being a prince.

"No, I can't stay, though I would like to. I have to

go back and get ready to rule my country. But I'll never forget you and some day we'll meet again, I'm sure of it."

With that he got into the big limousine and drove away, followed by the smaller car oozing bodyguards at every window. The three boys watched him go.

"For a prince, he seemed like a nice guy," Pete remarked. "Jupe—Jupe, what are you thinking about? You've got that look on your face!"

Jupiter blinked.

"I was wondering," he said. "Thinking back to this morning when we almost ran into Djaro's car, didn't anything strike you as strange about the incident?"

"Strange?" Bob sounded puzzled. "No, just lucky —lucky we didn't crash, that is."

"What are you getting at?" Pete asked.

"Markos, the driver of Djaro's car," Jupiter said. "He came out of that Stop street right in front of us. He must have seen us. But instead of speeding up to get out of our way, he put on the brakes. If Worthington wasn't a superb driver, we'd have crashed into the car exactly where Djaro was sitting. He'd probably have been killed."

"Markos just got rattled and did the wrong thing," Pete suggested.

"I wonder," Jupiter murmured. "Oh, well, I guess it isn't important. It was fun meeting Djaro. I don't suppose we'll ever see him again."

But Jupiter was wrong.

Chapter 2
A Surprising Invitation

Chapter 2

Standard Enumeration

SOME DAYS LATER, The Three Investigators were meeting in their Headquarters, the converted mobile home trailer hidden behind towering piles of lumber and scrap iron in The Jones Salvage Yard. Bob had just read a letter which had come in the morning mail from a lady in Malibu Beach who wanted them to find her missing dog when the telephone rang.

Their private phone, paid for out of their earnings helping Titus Jones at the salvage yard, didn't ring often. When it did, it always promised excitement. Jupiter grabbed it.

"Hello," he said. "Three Investigators, Jupiter Jones speaking."

"Good morning, young Jupiter." Alfred Hitchcock's rich voice boomed into the office from the loudspeaker Jupe had hooked up. "I'm glad to find you in. I wanted to let you know that you will shortly have a visitor."

"A visitor?" Jupe repeated. "About a case, sir?"

"I can tell you nothing," Alfred Hitchcock replied. "I am sworn to secrecy. However, I have had a long talk with your visitor and recommended you in the highest terms. You will receive a surprising invitation. That is all I can tell you. I just wanted to prepare you. Now I must say good-bye."

He hung up, and so did Jupiter. The three boys stared at each other.

"Do you suppose it's another case?" Bob asked.

They had no time to speculate, for at that moment Mathilda Jones' voice came booming in through the open skylight of Headquarters.

"Jupiter! Out front! You have a caller."

A moment later the boys were scrambling out through Tunnel Two, the big pipe which led from beneath the trailer to a hidden entrance in the workshop section of the yard. From there it took them only a moment to thread their way around piles of salvage material to the office.

A small car was parked there, and a young man stood beside it. They recognized him immediately. It was the American who had been part of Prince Djaro's escort the day they had almost collided with the foreign boy's car.

"Hello," he said, "I don't suppose you expected to see me again. This time let me introduce myself. I'm Bert Young, and here are my credentials."

He showed them an official-looking card, then slipped it back into his wallet.

"U. S. government—official business," he said. "Where can we talk in complete privacy?"

"Back here," Jupiter said, his eyes bulging a bit. A government agent and he wanted to talk to them in privacy! Also, he had been asking Mr. Hitchcock about them. What did it mean?

He led the way back to the workshop section and found two old chairs. Pete and Bob sat on a box.

"Maybe you've guessed why I'm here," Bert Young said. They hadn't, but they waited. "It's about Prince Djaro of Varania."

"Prince Djaro!" Bob exclaimed. "How is he?"

"He's fine and he sends his regards," Bert Young said. "I was talking to him just a couple of days ago. The point is, he wants you three to come visit him and stay for his coronation in two weeks."

"Wow!" Pete said. "Go all the way to Europe? Are you sure he wants *us?*"

"You and nobody else," Bert Young said. "Seems he felt you'd become real friends that day you all went to Disneyland. He hasn't many friends. Among the boys in Varania, he can't tell who's his friend and who's just buttering him up because he's the prince. But he's sure of you. He'd like some friends to be with him, and he wants you. I'll tell you the truth— I helped put the idea in his head."

"You did?" Bob asked. "Why?"

"Well," Bert Young said, "it's like this. Varania is a peaceful country. It's neutral, like Switzerland.

We, the United States, like it that way. That means it doesn't give any help to unfriendly countries."

"What help could a small nation like Varania give anyone?" Jupiter asked, speaking at last.

"You'd be surprised. It could let itself be a home base for spies, for one thing. But I can't go into that. The question is, will you go?"

The boys blinked. They certainly would like to go. But there were some difficulties. Their families, for one thing. And the expense, for another. Bert Young disposed of these swiftly.

"I'll talk to your families," he said. "I think I can convince them that you will be in good hands. First of all, I'll be there, and I'll keep an eye on you. And you'll be guests of the prince. As for expenses, we'll pay for your plane tickets. We'll also supply you with pocket money, because we want you to act like typical American kids—at least, as the Varanians imagine them. That means buying souvenirs and taking pictures."

Bob and Pete were too elated at this news to wonder at it. Jupiter, however, frowned.

"Why should the U. S. government do all this?" he asked. "Not just to be generous. Governments aren't generous that way."

"Alfred Hitchcock said you were smart." Bert Young grinned. "And I'm glad to see he's right. You see, fellows, the government wants you to act as junior agents while you're in Varania."

"You mean spy on Prince Djaro?" Pete asked indignantly.

Bert Young shook his head. "Absolutely not. But keep your eyes open. Watch everything that happens, and if you see or hear anything suspicious, report it immediately. The point is, something is stirring in Varania. We don't know what, and we think you can help us find out."

"That seems strange," Jupiter said, frowning. "I thought the government had sources of information that—"

"We're only human," Bert Young said. "And Varania is a hard place to learn anything. You see, the Varanians are so touchy and proud, they don't want help from any outside country. They're insulted if you offer it. They value their independence very highly.

"Just the same, we get rumors something is up. We have a feeling Duke Stefan, the Regent, isn't on the level. He's the ruler until Prince Djaro is crowned, and maybe he doesn't want Djaro crowned. Duke Stefan, the Prime Minister, and the entire Supreme Council, which is like our Congress, are a very tight little corporation. We feel they may do something to prevent Djaro from becoming prince.

"Now, ordinarily that would be a political matter and this country would keep its hands off. But the rumors say Duke Stefan has something bigger in mind. And that's as far as they go. We need to know what he's up to. Just maybe, if you're living right there in the palace, you can find out for us. None of the rest of us can get close enough to the Varanians to learn the truth. Maybe Djaro knows something and is too proud to ask for help, but will tell you. Or maybe the others, thinking you're just ordinary kids, will get careless and let something slip.

"The big question is, will you accept the assignment?"

Bob and Pete waited for Jupiter, as head of the firm, to speak. Jupe thought for a moment, then he nodded.

"If what you want us to do is try to help Prince Djaro, we'll do it," he said. "That is, if our families will let us. But we told Djaro we'd be his friends and we won't do anything against him."

"That's what I wanted to hear!" Bert Young exclaimed. "Only one caution. Don't tell Djaro you know there's something wrong. Get him to tell you if possible. And don't let anyone guess why you're there. Almost all the Varanians are loyal to Djaro —they adored his father, who was killed in a hunting accident eight years ago. And they don't much like Duke Stefan. But if they thought you were spying, even in a good cause, they'd raise a terrific ruckus. So keep your eyes and ears open and your mouths shut.

"Got that? All right, fellows, let's get this show on the road!"

Chapter 3
The Silver Spider

VARANIA! Bob stood on the stone balcony and looked out across the rooftops of the ancient city of Denzo. In the morning sunshine the city was a mass of waving treetops, pierced by tiled roofs and the tall towers of public buildings. The golden dome of a great church rose from a small hill about half a mile away. In the stone-paved courtyard below, scrub-women with buckets and brushes were shining the very stones.

Behind the five-story stone palace the Denzo River, broad and swift, wound through the city. Small excursion boats moved slowly along the river. It was a very colorful scene, and from the balcony of their third-floor corner room, Bob had an excellent view.

"It's certainly different from California," Pete said, stepping out through the French doors to join Bob on the balcony. "You can tell just by looking at it this city is old."

"Founded in 1335," Bob said. He had, of course,

read up on Varania and its history in the hectic days before he and Pete and Jupiter had set out on their exciting journey. "Invaded several times and destroyed, but always rebuilt. It's been at peace since 1675 when Prince Paul put down a rebellion and became the big national hero, like our George Washington. Everything we're looking at is about three hundred years old. There's a modern section to the city, but it's out of sight over that way."

"I like it," Pete said admiringly. "How much country is there to go along with the city?"

"Only about fifty square miles," Bob told him. "It really is a small nation. See those hills in the distance? Varania's border is at the top of them. The country runs about seven miles up the Denzo River. Grape-growing, making fine textiles, and entertaining visitors are the principal industries. Lots of tourists come here because it's very picturesque. Because of the tourists, most of the shopkeepers still wear the old Varanian costumes. To give it atmosphere."

Jupiter Jones, buttoning a bright sport shirt, stepped out of their room and surveyed the view admiringly.

"It looks like a movie set," he said. "Except that it's real. What's that church over there, Bob?"

"I guess it must be St. Dominic's," Bob said. "That's the biggest church and the only one that has a golden dome and two bell towers. See those tall spires? They have bells in them. The tower on the left has eight bells that ring for church services and

on national holidays. The one on the right has one big old monster of a bell that is called Prince Paul's bell. When Prince Paul put down the rebellion in 1675, he rang it to let his loyal followers know he was alive and needed help. They rallied around and chased the rebels out. Since then it has been rung only for the royal family.

"When a prince is crowned, it rings one hundred times, very slowly. When a prince is born, it rings fifty times and when a princess is born, twenty-five times. For a royal wedding it rings seventy-five times. It has a very deep note, unlike any other bell in the city, and can be heard for at least three miles."

"Good old Records!" Pete grinned.

"We ought to be getting ready to see Djaro," Jupiter put in. "The Royal Chamberlain said Djaro would join us for breakfast."

"Speaking of breakfast, I could use some," Pete exclaimed. "I wonder where we'll eat?"

"We'll have to wait and see," Jupiter answered. "Let's check our equipment and make sure everything's in order. After all, we're here on business."

He led the way back into the room. It had high ceilings and paneled walls that had a deep satin glow to them. Over the bed, which was more than six feet wide and in which all three had slept, was a carved coat of arms of Djaro's family.

Their bags still stood on a stand. They had opened them only to get out pajamas and toothbrushes when they arrived late the previous evening. A jet had flown them to New York, and from there to Paris. However, they had seen nothing of either city, for they had not left the airport. At Paris, they had changed to a big helicopter which flew them to Denzo's tiny airport.

Then an automobile had taken them to the palace and the Royal Chamberlain had greeted them. Djaro was at a special meeting and unable to see them, he had said, but would join them for breakfast. He had led them through positively miles of stone corridors, to come at last to this bedroom. They had tumbled into bed and fallen asleep immediately, without unpacking.

Now they unpacked and put away their clothes.

When they had put their things in a roomy clothes cabinet that looked about five hundred years old— closets had been unknown when the castle was built —they looked at the three items they had left out.

Three cameras. At least they looked like cameras. And they were cameras, rather large and expensive looking, with flashbulb attachments and plenty of gadgets. But you could also use them as radios. Very special, high-power walkie-talkie equipment was built into the back of each camera. The flashbulb attachment doubled as an antenna for sending and receiving. You could speak into the camera, and your voice would travel as far as ten miles. Even from inside a building the range was a couple of miles.

The walkie-talkies had only two communication bands, and they couldn't be picked up by any radio or walkie-talkie except one tuned to the same channels. The only such radios, aside from the three that lay on the bed now, were in the American Embassy where Bert Young was.

He had flown with them from Los Angeles to New York, and all the way had talked to them earnestly. Among other things he had said that he would never be too far away from them, and would expect them to communicate with him by camera walkie-talkie every night. Sooner, if something important happened.

"Now understand me, fellows," he had said, "maybe everything will go smoothly and Prince Djaro will be crowned according to schedule. But I think there's trouble brewing and I hope you can help us spot it.

"Don't ask questions—as I told you, the Varanians don't want anyone prying into their business. Just wander around and take pictures of the scenery, and keep your eyes and ears open. You'll be reporting to me regularly on the camera-radios. I'll have a listening post, probably at the American Embassy.

"That's all for now. After you get on the plane for Paris you're on your own, except for radio contact. I'll get to Varania on a different plane and be ready for you. Any further plans we'll have to make as things develop. For code purposes when you report, you'll be First, Second, and Records. Got it?"

With that Bert Young had wiped his brow, and they had felt like wiping theirs. It was a rather frightening assignment. To all intents and purposes they were secret agents working for the U. S. government.

Now, remembering all Bert Young had told them, they felt rather subdued. Pete was the first to break the silence. He picked up his camera and opened the leather case in which it was carried. In the bottom of the leather case was still another gadget—a very tiny transistorized tape recorder that could pick up conversation from across a room.

"Before we see Djaro," he said, "shouldn't we contact Mr. Young? Just to make sure everything's working?"

"A good idea, Second," Jupiter agreed. "I'll step out on the balcony and take a picture of the view."

He picked up his camera and trotted out to the balcony. Opening the leather case, he focused on the golden dome of St. Dominic's.

He pressed down on the button that activated the walkie-talkie.

"First reporting," he said softly, bending over the camera, apparently to study the picture in the view finder. "First reporting, do you read me?"

Almost instantly a voice that could not be heard three feet away answered.

"I read you," Bert Young said. "Anything to report?"

"Just testing. We haven't seen Prince Djaro yet. We're due to meet him for breakfast."

"I'll be standing by. Keep alert. Over and out."

"Roger," Jupe said and came back into the room just as a knock sounded on the door.

Pete opened it and there stood Prince Djaro, beaming at them.

"My friends! Pete! Bob! Jupiter!" he exclaimed and threw his arms around them warmly, in a European-style greeting. "I'm glad to see you! What do you think of my country and my city? But you haven't had much time to see them, have you? We'll take care of that soon—as soon as we've all had breakfast."

He turned and signaled with his hand.

"Come in," he directed. "Set the table by the window."

Eight servants, wearing the royal livery of gold and scarlet, brought in a table, chairs, and several platters with silver covers on them. Djaro kept up a stream of cheerful talk while the servitors set up the table, put a snowy white linen cloth on it, set it with heavy silver, and then uncovered plates of eggs and bacon and sausage, toast and waffles, and glasses of milk.

"That looks good!" Pete exclaimed. "I'm starved."

"Sure thing," Djaro said. "Let's all eat. Come on, Bob, what are you looking at?"

Bob was staring at a large spider web which had been spun from the head of the bed to the corner of the room about two feet away. A big spider peered at him from a crack between the floor and the wainscoting. Bob was thinking that Djaro had a lot of servants but the maids weren't very tidy.

"I just noticed that spider web," he said. "I'll brush it off."

He started toward it. To the boys' amazement, Prince Djaro hurled himself at Bob's legs and in a flying tackle brought him to the floor just before he could sweep away the spider web.

Pete and Jupe looked on in astonishment as Djaro helped Bob to his feet. He was speaking rapidly.

"I should have warned you sooner, Bob," he said. "But I haven't had time. Thank goodness I stopped you from destroying that spider web. I would have had to send you home at once. As it is, I am very happy to see it. It is a good omen. It means you will be able to help me."

He dropped his voice as if someone might be listening. Then he strode to the door and flung it suddenly open. A red-jacketed man was standing there at attention, looking very impressive with black hair and a tightly curled black mustache.

"Yes, Bilkis, what is it?" Djaro demanded.

"I merely waited in case Your Highness wished something," the man said.

"Nothing now. Leave us. Return in half an hour for the dishes," Djaro barked. The man bowed again, turned away and strode down the long hall.

Djaro closed the door. Then he came close to them and spoke in a low voice.

"One of Duke Stefan's men. He may have been

spying on us. I have something very important to talk to you about. I need your help. The silver spider of Varania has been stolen!"

Chapter 4
Djaro Explains

" I H A V E a lot to tell you," Djaro said, "so we'd better eat first. It'll be easier talking afterwards."

So eat they did, until they were stuffed. Then the servitors came and removed the table, chairs, and dishes. After making sure that Bilkis was not lurking again in the corridor, Djaro pulled up chairs close to the window and began to talk.

"I have to tell you something of the history of Varania," he said. "In 1675, when Prince Paul was about to be crowned ruler, there was a revolution and he had to hide. He took refuge in the home of a humble family of minstrels, street singers who earned their living by entertaining in public.

"At the risk of their lives, they hid Prince Paul in the attic of their home. He would surely have been found, for his enemies searched high and low for him, except for the fact that a spider built a web across the trap door almost immediately after he went through. Thus it looked as if it had not been touched for days.

The revolutionists saw it and did not bother to look into the attic.

"For three days Prince Paul hid there without food or water. The family of minstrels could not feed him without opening the trap door and disturbing the spider web, you see, and that was what protected him. In the end my ancestor emerged, rang the bell we now call the bell of Prince Paul to summon his followers, and drove the rebels from the city.

"When he ascended the throne, he wore about his neck an emblem created for him by the nation's finest silversmith—a silver spider on a silver chain. He proclaimed the spider Varania's national mascot and the royal symbol of the reigning family, and decreed that henceforth no prince should be crowned unless he wore around his neck the silver spider of Prince Paul.

"From that day the spider has been a symbol of good luck in Varania. Housewives are glad when one builds its web in their homes. The webs are not disturbed and no one would injure a spider deliberately."

"You could never get my mother to go along with that!" Pete exclaimed. "She's death on spider webs. She thinks spiders are dirty and poisonous."

"On the contrary," Jupiter spoke up, "spiders are very clean creatures, frequently cleansing themselves like tiny cats. And while the black widow spider is somewhat poisonous, it only bites if you practically make it do so. Even the big spiders, the tarantulas, are not nearly as dangerous as popularly supposed. In tests they have had to be teased to make them bite anyone. Most spiders, especially in this part of the world, are harmless and do a lot of good by catching other insects."

"That is true," Prince Djaro said. "Here in Varania there are no harmful spiders. The one we call Prince Paul's spider is the largest species we have, and it is very handsome. It is black with gold markings, and usually builds its web out of doors, but sometimes it comes inside. That web you almost brushed away, Bob, belongs to a Prince Paul spider. It is an omen that you have come to bring me help in my difficulty."

"Well, I'm glad you stopped me from brushing it off," Bob said. "But what is your trouble?"

Djaro hesitated. Then he shook his head.

"No one knows this but myself," he said. "Unless, as I am sure, Duke Stefan knows. A new prince of Varania, by long tradition, must wear the silver spider of Prince Paul when he is crowned. So I must wear it around my neck two weeks from now when I'm crowned. And I can't."

"Why can't you?" Pete asked.

"Djaro means because it has been stolen," Jupe put in. "Is that it, Djaro?"

Djaro nodded emphatically.

"It has been stolen and a substitute put in its place. But the substitute won't do. Unless I can find the real silver spider soon, I can't be crowned on sched-

ule. There will be an inquiry, a scandal. And if that
happens—but no, I will not speak of that.

"I know this seems to you like a lot of fuss about a
little piece of jewelry. But the silver spider means to
us of Varania what the crown jewels mean to the
English. No, more—for it is the emblem of the royal
family, and no one else in Varania may make or
own an imitation spider. Except for the Order of the
Silver Spider, which is bestowed upon a Varanian for
the highest service to his country.

"We are a small country, but we have old
traditions and we cling to them in this modern age of
change. Perhaps we cling to them more strongly because so much is changing all around us. You are investigators. You are also my friends. Do you think
you can find the real silver spider for me?"

Jupiter pinched his lower lip thoughtfully.

"I don't know, Djaro," he said. "Is this silver spider life-size?"

Djaro nodded. "About as large as an American
quarter."

"Then that means it's very small. It could be hidden anywhere. Maybe it has been destroyed."

"I do not think so," Djaro told him. "No, I am sure
it has not been destroyed. It is too important for that.
As for its being easy to hide, what you say is true. Yet
if anyone is hiding it, he must be very careful he is
not found with it, for that could mean death. Even
for Duke Stefan."

Prince Djaro took a deep breath.

"Well," he said, "I've told you. I haven't any idea how you can help me, but I only hope you can. Somehow. That is why, when someone suggested perhaps I would like to have my American friends visit me for the coronation, I leaped at the idea. Now you are here. But no one knows you are investigators, and no one must know. Anything you do you must do as— well, just as American boys." Djaro searched their faces. "What do you think? Can you aid me?"

"I don't know," Jupiter said honestly. "Finding a little silver spider that could be hidden anywhere is very difficult. But we can try. First I think we ought to see where it was stolen from and what it looks like. You said there was an imitation in its place?"

"Yes, a very good imitation, but just an imitation. Come. I'll show you right away. I'll take you to the room of relics."

The three grabbed their cameras and Djaro led them through a long stone corridor. They went down some winding steps to a broader corridor below. The walls, floors and ceilings were all of stone.

"The palace was built nearly three hundred years ago," Djaro told them. "The foundations and part of the walls belonged to an old castle that used to stand here. There are dozens of empty rooms—in fact, no one ever goes into the upper two floors. Varania is a poor country and we can't afford all the servants it would take to keep the whole palace open. Besides, there is no heat except for the rooms that have been modernized, and we could not afford to modernize very much of it. Imagine living here without heat!"

They could imagine it easily. Although it was August, it was very cool inside Djaro's palace.

"There are dungeons and cellars left over from the old castle," continued Djaro, as they went down another flight of stairs, "with secret entrances we've forgotten about, and secret stairways that lead nowhere. Even I could get lost if I wandered away from the parts I'm used to."

He laughed now. "It would be a great place for a horror movie," he said, "with ghosts dodging in and out of the secret entrances. Luckily, we have no ghosts. Uh-oh!" he added. "Here comes Duke Stefan."

As they reached the lower corridor, a tall man came hurrying along. He stopped and made a little bow to Djaro.

"Good morning, Djaro," he said. "These are your American friends?"

His voice was chilly and formal. He himself was straight as a spear, with a drooping black mustache and a hawk nose.

"Good morning, Duke Stefan," replied Djaro. "These are my friends, yes. Let me present Jupiter Jones, Peter Crenshaw, and Bob Andrews, all from California in the United States."

The tall man inclined his head an inch at each introduction. His sharp eyes inspected them carefully.

"Welcome to Varania," he said, in the same polite but chilly tone. "You are showing your friends the castle?"

"We're going to the relic room," Djaro said. "They are interested in the history of our nation. Duke Stefan," he told the boys, "is Regent of Varania. He has ruled since my father was killed in a hunting accident."

"In your name, Prince," Duke Stefan said quickly. "And for your benefit, I hope. I will accompany you. It is only fitting that I show courtesy to your guests."

"Very well," Djaro answered, though The Three Investigators could tell it was the last thing he wanted. "But we must not take you from your duties for too long. I believe you have a council meeting this morning, Duke Stefan?"

"Yes," the man answered, falling into step beside them. "To consider the details of your coronation, which happy event will take place in two weeks. But I can spare a few moments."

Djaro said nothing more but led them down the corridor until they reached a large room with a ceiling two stories high. Pictures covered the walls, and the room was full of glass cases. In them were old flags, shields, medals, books and other relics. Each had a neatly typed white card beside it telling what it was. The boys peered into a case containing a broken sword. The card said it was the sword used by Prince Paul in successfully combating the revolution of 1675.

"Here in this room," Duke Stefan said, "is a condensed history of our nation. But we are a small nation, and our history has not been an exciting one.

You no doubt find us rather quaint and old-fashioned, coming from the vast country of America."

"No, sir," Jupiter said politely. "From what we have seen of your country so far it is very attractive."

"Most of your countrymen," Duke Stefan said, "find us hopelessly impractical and behind the times. I only hope our slow pace will not bore you. However, you must excuse me now. I have to attend the council meeting."

He turned on his heel and strode off.

Bob gave a little sigh of relief. "He didn't like us, that's for certain," he said in a low voice.

"Because you are my friends," Djaro said. "And he does not want me to have friends. He does not want me to speak up and oppose him, as I have been doing lately—especially since visiting America. But let's forget him. Look, here is a picture of Prince Paul himself."

He led them to a life-size painting of a man wearing a brilliant red uniform with gold buttons, a sword held in one hand so the point touched the floor. He had a noble face and an eagle gaze. His other hand was outstretched, and on it sat a spider. The boys examined it closely. It was really very handsome, with a velvety black body specked with gold.

"My ancestor," Djaro said proudly. "Prince Paul the Conqueror. And the spider that saved his life."

As the boys studied the picture, they could hear voices behind them in many languages, including English. The room was quite crowded with people,

most of them obviously tourists. They carried cameras or guidebooks, or both. Two royal guards were stationed in the room, standing at attention, each of them holding a spear.

One American couple, a rather stout man and his wife, took up positions just behind the four.

"Ugh!" they heard the woman say. "Look at that nasty old spider!"

"Sssh!" the man cautioned. "Don't let these people hear you say that. That's their good-luck mascot. Besides, spiders are much nicer than they're given credit for. It's just a case of getting a bad name."

"I don't care," the woman answered. "If I see one I'm going to step on it."

Pete and Bob grinned. Djaro's eyes twinkled. Little by little the boys made their way around the room until they came to a door at which a third guard stood at attention.

"I wish to enter, Sergeant," Djaro said. The soldier saluted respectfully.

"Yes, sire," he said.

He stood to one side and Djaro produced a key which opened the heavy, brass-studded door. Inside was a short hall. At the end of it they saw another door, locked with a combination lock. Djaro opened this, and beyond it was still a third door, this one of iron grillwork. When this was finally unlocked, they stepped into a room about eight feet square which looked like, and really was, a bank vault.

Next to one wall were glass cabinets displaying the

royal jewels—a crown, a scepter, and several neck-laces and rings.

"For the queen—when there is a queen," Djaro said, pointing to the jewelry. "We don't have many jewels—we're not rich—but we guard them well, as you can see. However, this is what we want to look at."

He led the way to a cabinet by itself in the center of the room. Here on a special stand reposed a spider on a silver chain. To the amazement of the three boys, it looked exactly like the real thing.

"It is enamel over silver," Djaro explained. "You thought it would be all silver? No, it is black enamel with specks of gold. The eyes are small rubies. But it is not the genuine silver spider of Varania. That is far superior to this one."

The jeweled spider looked like a first-class job to the boys, but they accepted Djaro's word for it. They studied it from all angles so they could recognize the original if they had the luck to find it.

"The real one was taken last week, and this imita-tion left in its place," Djaro said bitterly. "I suspect the only man who could have done it—Duke Ste-fan. But I cannot speak without proof. The political situation is very delicate. All the members of the Supreme Council are Stefan's men. Until I am crowned I have little power, and they do not want me crowned. The theft of the royal spider is the first step to prevent me from taking my place as ruler.

"But I cannot bore you with so many details. Besides, I have to go to a meeting myself. I will take you back outside and leave you. There is a car and a driver ready—you can go sightseeing in the city. I will see you tonight, after dinner, and we will talk again."

He led them out of the jewel vault, locking all the doors. Once outside the relic room he shook their hands, and told them where to find the car that was waiting.

"The driver's name is Rudy," he said. "He is faithful to me. I would like to go with you," he added wistfully. "Being a prince is often dull. But I must be what I am. Enjoy yourselves and we will talk tonight."

He walked rapidly away down the corridor.

Bob scratched his head. "What do you think, Jupe?" he asked. "Can we find Djaro's royal spider for him?"

Jupiter sighed. "I don't see how," he said. "Not unless we have an awful lot of luck."

Chapter 5
A Sinister Conversation

T H E Three Investigators enjoyed their drive through the capital city of Varania. To boys who had been brought up in California, where everything was new, it was unbelievably old. Even the apartment houses were made of stone, or else a kind of yellow brick. Many of the roofs were of red slate, and there were squares and fountains every block or so. Flocks of pigeons strutted everywhere—especially in front of St. Dominic's cathedral.

Their car was an ancient open touring car, and their driver a young man in a smart uniform who spoke English well. His name was Rudy, and he informed them in a low voice that they could trust him, that he was loyal to Prince Djaro.

They drove into the hills ouside Denzo to see the view of the river from the heights. As they were climbing back into the car after taking some pictures, Rudy spoke in a low tone.

"We are being followed," he said. "We have been followed ever since we left the palace. I am going to drive you to the park now, and you may walk through it and watch the entertainers. But don't look back. Don't let them know they've been spotted!"

Not look back! It was a hard order to obey. Who was following them? And why?

"I wish I knew more about what's going on," Pete grumbled as they drove back through the colorful streets. "Why would anybody follow us? We don't know anything!"

"Someone may think we do," Jupiter suggested.

"Someone wishes we did," Bob added. "Me."

Rudy pulled the car to a stop. They had reached a large, tree-covered square where many people were strolling. Faintly they could hear the sound of music.

"This is our main park," Rudy said, leaping out to open the door for them. "Walk slowly to the center, past the bandstand. When you reach the entertainers, the tumblers and clowns, take some pictures. Then ask the girl who sells balloons to let you take her picture. She is my sister, Elena. I will wait here for you until you get back. Oh, and don't look behind you. You'll probably be followed but you don't need to be worried. At least not yet."

"At least not yet!" Pete said as they walked slowly beneath the trees in the direction of the music. "Well, that gives us something to look forward to."

"How can we possibly help Djaro?" Bob wanted to know. "It's all a wild goose chase. We can't do anything."

"We have to wait for developments," Jupiter said. "My guess is we're being followed to see if we contact anyone. Bert Young, for instance."

They walked on a little further and came to an open area where many people were sitting on the grass. On a tiny bandstand a band of eight men in brilliant uniforms tootled loudly. They finished and everyone applauded. As if this was a signal to try even harder, the band immediately started another tune.

The Three Investigators circled around the bandstand and kept walking. There were many people strolling along the paths so they could not tell if they were being followed. Presently they came to a wide paved area.

Here were the entertainers Rudy had mentioned. A trampoline had been set up and two tumblers were doing fantastic leaps and somersaults on it. A couple of clowns did flip-flops on the ground among the passers-by, holding out little baskets into which most of the strollers good-naturedly dropped a coin.

A very attractive girl in a native peasant costume stood nearby with a huge bunch of balloons. As she sold them she sang a song in English about buying a balloon to set it free, so it could carry your wishes up to the sky. Many people did buy balloons and set them free, and they shot upward, colorful globes of red and yellow and blue, until they disappeared.

"Take pictures of the clowns, Pete," Jupiter directed. "I'll get some shots of the acrobats. Bob, you just sort of look around to see if you notice anything."

"Right, First." Pete walked over in the direction of a tumbling clown.

Jupiter, with Bob at his elbow, opened his camera and focused it on the tumblers. He fussed with it, seeming to have trouble. Actually, he was pressing down the lever that activated the powerful walkie-talkie.

"First here," he said in a low voice. "Do you read me?"

"Coming in loud and clear," Bert Young's voice murmured back from the camera. "What's the situation?"

"We're sightseeing," Jupiter said. "Prince Djaro has asked us to help him recover the royal spider of Varania. It has been stolen and a substitute left in its place."

"Uh-oh!" Bert Young exclaimed. "That's worse than I thought. Can you help him?"

"I don't see how," Jupe admitted.

"Neither do I," Bert Young agreed. "But stay with it and keep your eyes open. Anything else?"

"We're in the park and we've probably been followed. We don't know by whom."

"Try to get a look at them. Report back to me later, but wait until you're alone. Someone may get suspicious if you talk now."

With that Bert Young broke off. Jupiter took his pictures, while Bob looked slowly all around. Seeing nothing—that is, no one who looked like he was shadowing them—he dropped some American coins into a clown's basket.

Now the clowns led out a French poodle, who did somersaults and stood on his front legs. The crowd gathered around to watch, leaving the balloon girl free for the moment.

"Now we take a picture of the girl," Jupiter murmured to the others. They all moved over, Jupiter focusing his camera. The girl saw him, smiled, and posed. Jupiter snapped the picture. Then the girl came forward with her balloons.

"Buy a balloon, young American gentlemen?" she said. "Set it free, let it soar into the clouds and take your wish up to heaven."

Pete found some American money and gave it to her. She handed each of them a balloon and then turned to the task of making change. As she bent over the coins, she whispered beneath her breath.

"You are being followed. A man and a woman. They do not look dangerous. I think they want to talk to you. Sit down at a table over there and order ice cream. Give them a chance to talk to you."

The boys each made a wish and released their balloons. They watched them till they were tiny dots in the sky. Then they strolled over to a space where a number of tables with checkered red cloths stood on the grass. They sat down at one and a waiter with a handlebar mustache hurried over and said, "Ice cream? Maybe hot chocolate? Sandwiches?"

They nodded, and the waiter bustled off. Looking around, they saw a man and a woman buying balloons. Bob recognized them as the same couple who had stood behind them looking at the portrait of Prince Paul that morning. And he felt sure it was they who had been doing the following.

Slowly, the two strolled over and selected the table next to the boys. They ordered ice cream and coffee, then leaned back and smiled at Pete, Bob and Jupiter.

"Aren't you boys Americans?" the woman asked, in a rather husky voice.

"Yes, ma'am," Jupiter answered. "Are you Americans, too?"

"We certainly are," the woman said. "From California, just like you."

Jupe stiffened. How did the couple know they were from California? The man said quickly, "You *are* from California, aren't you? Anyway, you're wearing California-style sport shirts."

"Yes, sir," Jupiter said, "We're from California. We just arrived last night."

"We saw you this morning in the relic room at the castle," the woman said. "Dear me, wasn't that Prince Djaro himself who was with you?"

Jupiter nodded. "Yes, he was showing us around." Then he turned to Bob and Pete. "I think we ought to wash up before the waiter brings our lunch," he said.

"I saw a sign pointing to the washroom, over beyond the tumblers."

He turned to the couple at the next table.

"We're going to wash up," he told them. "I wonder if you'd watch our cameras for us while we're gone."

"Sure thing, sonny." The man gave him a big smile. "Don't worry, we won't let them get stolen."

"Thank you, sir." Jupiter rose, not giving Bob or Pete a chance to say anything, and started off in the direction of the washroom. The other two hastily followed him.

"What's the idea, Jupe?" Pete whispered as they caught up with him. "Why go off and leave our cameras?"

"Sssh!" Jupe cautioned. "I have an idea. Just come along."

They passed close to the girl selling balloons, and without pausing Jupiter said softly: "Please watch the man and woman. If they touch our cameras, let us know. We'll be back in a minute."

She nodded, and The Three Investigators sauntered on as if they were ordinary, carefree sightseers.

The washroom was a stone building inconspicuously placed in a grove of trees. They found themselves alone inside and Pete burst out, "What's your idea, Jupe?"

"Those two," Jupiter told him, turning on a faucet. "They may talk while we're away. They may let something slip."

"But what good will that do us?" Bob asked, joining him in washing his hands.

"I left the tape recorder inside my camera going," Jupe told him. "It's very sensitive. It'll pick up anything they say. Now we better not talk any more. Someone might overhear us."

They finished washing up in silence, then walked slowly back to their table. As they passed the balloon seller, she shook her head once. Apparently nothing had happened while they were gone. Their cameras were still on the table, and the man and woman were sipping coffee.

"Nobody tried to bother your cameras, boys," the man said genially. "This is a very honest country. The waiter brought your order, but we told him you'd be gone for a minute. Ah, here he comes now."

The waiter approached with a loaded tray, and set down sandwiches, hot chocolate and ice cream. Realizing they wouldn't have any other lunch, the trio ate hungrily. After a few minutes the man and woman at the next table finished, said good-bye, and walked away.

"If they intended to talk to us, they changed their minds," Pete remarked.

"I'm hoping they talked to each other," Jupiter said. He touched a tiny button on his camera. This rewound the tape in the tape recorder, and at the touch of another button the tape began to play. At first there were just faint hisses. Then the man's voice spoke. Bob jumped with excitement.

"It worked!" he exclaimed. "Just as you figured, Jupe."

"Sssh!" Jupe quieted him. "Let's listen to what was said. Keep on eating. Don't look at the camera."

He rewound the tape and started it over again, adjusting the volume control lever so the voices could not be heard even at the next table.

They heard the following conversation:

Man: "I think Freddie sent us on a wild goose chase. If those three kids are investigators I'll eat my hat."

Woman: "Freddie isn't wrong very often. He said those are three smart boys. He's checked up on them. Call themselves The Three Investigators."

Man: "Just playacting! You can't tell me they ever solved anything except by dumb luck. Why, if I ever saw a stupid-looking kid, it's that fat one." (At this Pete and Bob suppressed chuckles with difficulty. Jupe had been trying to look stupid, but even so he didn't much care for the comment.)

Woman: "Just the same, Freddie said to follow them and see if they contact anyone. He thinks they're working with the CIA."

Man: "They don't know anything to tell anybody. They're just wandering around like any kids. Let someone else follow them."

Woman: "You aren't going to try to talk them into persuading the prince to go along with Duke Stefan's plans?"

Man: "No, I don't think that's a good idea. I think

the only thing to do is what Freddie's been for all along. Throw the prince out, and get Duke Stefan made permanent Regent. Then, through our hold on Stefan, our syndicate and Roberto's will be the actual rulers of this country."

Woman: "You'd better lower your voice. Someone might hear you."

Man: "There's no one around to hear. I tell you, Mabel, this is the most perfect setup anyone ever dreamed of. Once we take over, with Duke Stefan acting as front for us, we'll really cut loose. Did you ever stop to think what you could do if you owned your own country?"

Woman: "Gambling, you said. We'll make this country bigger than Monte Carlo for that."

Man: "Yes. Then there's banking. We'll offer safe banking privileges for people in the States who want to hide money where the government can't find it. But that's only the beginning. We'll repeal all extradition laws. That means other governments won't be able to arrest criminals who take refuge here. Anybody wanted for anything anywhere in the world will be safe here—as long as he can pay our price. Varania will be heaven for crooks on the run."

Woman: "It sounds perfect. But what if Duke Stefan doesn't go along with our plans?"

Man: "He has to, if he wants to stay in power. We've got the goods on him. Oh, I tell you, Varania is a sweet, juicy pear and all we have to do is pick it."

Woman: "Sssh! Here they come back."

The tape went dead. Jupiter casually turned the camera around, in doing so switching off the tape and rewinding it.

"Golly!" Pete said. "It's as bad as Bert Young feared. Worse! They plan to turn this whole country into a crooks' paradise."

"We've got to tell Bert Young!" Bob exclaimed.

Jupiter frowned. "I think we should," he said. "I'd like to play him the whole tape, but that would take too long. Someone might notice. We'll give him the gist of it, though."

He picked up the camera and pretended to be changing the film. He switched on the transmitting lever and spoke softly.

"First reporting," he said. "Can you read me?"

"Loud and clear," Bert Young's voice came back. "New developments?"

Jupiter told him what had happened, as briefly as he could.

"That's bad," Bert Young said when he had finished. "The man and woman you describe sound like Max Grogan, a gambler from Nevada, and his wife. They're part of a big crime syndicate in the States. The Freddie and Roberto they mentioned must be Freddie 'Fingers' McGraw and Roberto Roulette, both of them big-time gamblers. This whole thing is far bigger than we dreamed—nothing less than an attempt by crooks to take over the kingdom of Varania.

"You'll have to warn Prince Djaro, first chance you get. Then tomorrow come to the American Embassy.

The castle may not be safe any longer. We'll try to help Djaro if he'll just let us, but we have to wait for a request from him.

"You've done fine so far—more than we dreamed you could. But from now on, be careful!"

Chapter 6
A Startling Discovery

THE Three Investigators spent the rest of the afternoon sightseeing. They visited some quaint old shops, and an interesting museum. Then they took a ride up the river on a small excursion steamer.

Rudy reported from time to time that they were still being followed. However, now it was by members of the Varanian secret service, really in the employ of Duke Stefan.

"Perhaps they are just looking after you," Rudy said darkly, "but I doubt it. They are interested in you. And I wish I knew why."

The boys wished they knew why, too. There didn't seem any reason why anyone should be interested in them. They had done nothing yet, and certainly hadn't been able to help Prince Djaro at all.

From time to time they passed small groups of people playing musical instruments on street corners.

"Minstrels," Rudy told them. "All descendants of the family that sheltered Prince Paul many years ago. I, too, am one, though my father used to be prime minister until Duke Stefan discharged him. We are Prince Djaro's most faithful subjects, for by Prince Paul's decree we pay no taxes.

"We have formed a secret party opposed to Duke Stefan. We call ourselves the Minstrel Party, or just Minstrels. The people do not like Duke Stefan, I can tell you."

Each time they passed a group of Minstrels, Rudy slowed the car slightly. Then, when one of the musicians gave him a slight nod, he speeded up again.

"Two can play at this game," he muttered. "We are watching those who watch you. We shall be keeping an eye on you at all times. We have our people in the palace, too, even in the Royal Guard. We know much. But we do not know why you have become so important to them. I suspect a plot of some kind, and Duke Stefan's plots are apt to be very nasty ones."

They kept on sightseeing, and gradually forgot about the shadowers. They rode on a majestic merry-go-round in the park, and ate dinner at an outdoor restaurant that specialized in fine fish from the river.

They rode back to the castle rather tired, but feeling full and comfortable.

The Royal Chamberlain, a rotund little man in a scarlet robe, hurried up to greet them.

"Good evening, young gentlemen," he said. "Prince Djaro is sorry he cannot see you tonight but will breakfast with you in the morning again. I shall lead you to your room, for I fear you cannot find it by yourselves."

He led them up a bewildering succession of stairs and halls, past many footmen, to their room. As soon as they entered he scurried away, as if on some important errand.

They closed the stout oak door and looked around the room. It had been tidied up and their bed made, but their suitcases were where they had left them. Bob noticed that the big spider web was still in place in the corner by the head of the bed. A large black and gold spider scurried for cover as they came in, and hid in the small crack between floor and wainscoting.

Bob grinned. By now he had accepted the fact that spiders were practically sacred in Varania, and had decided they were even rather handsome when you examined them closely.

"Nothing new has happened," Jupiter said, "but I think we'd better contact Mr. Young. He might have some instructions. As a precaution, Pete, you might lock the door."

Pete turned the lock on the door. Jupiter unslung his camera, and pushed the sending lever.

"First reporting," he said. "Do you read me?"

"Loud and clear," came back Bert Young's answering voice. "Any more developments?"

"Nothing special," Jupiter said. "We went sightseeing. But we were followed all day by Duke Stefan's secret service."

"He's worried about you," Bert Young said thoughtfully. "Have you spoken to Djaro yet? How did he take the news?"

"We haven't been able to see him. The Royal Chamberlain said he couldn't see us until morning."

"Hmm." Over the radio they could almost hear Bert Young thinking. "I wonder if they are keeping him away from you on purpose. It's vitally important that you see him in the morning and tell him. Now take that tape out of the camera and put it in your pocket. I want you to bring it to me tomorrow here at the Embassy. Just leave as if you're sightseeing and have your driver bring you here. Things are apt to get hot from now on. Understand?"

"Yes, sir," Jupe answered.

"We're still trying to figure out how to help Prince Djaro. Duke Stefan has such tight control over the radio, the newspapers, and television, we can't reach the people that way. But we'll figure something. So as of tomorrow you're relieved from duty."

"Yes, sir," Jupiter agreed. "Over and out."

He turned off the transmitter switch, opened the bottom of the camera, and took out a tiny spool of tape.

"Here, Pete," he said, "you carry this. Don't let anyone get it away from you."

"Right," Pete said and put the tape in an inside pocket.

While Jupe was talking to Bert Young, Bob had been rummaging in a drawer of the big wardrobe for a handkerchief. He found his handkerchiefs where he had put them, but as he pulled one out he heard a small clinking sound. Curious, he felt to see what caused it. There was something heavy and metallic hidden under his handkerchiefs. He pulled it out, stared at it and gave a yell.

"Jupe! Pete! Look!"

They turned in surprise.

"A spider!" Pete gulped. "Drop it!"

"It's harmless," Jupiter said. "It's a Prince Paul spider. Put it on the floor, Bob."

"You don't understand!" Bob exclaimed. "It's not *a* spider. It's *the* spider!"

"*The* spider?" Pete repeated. "What do you mean?"

"The silver spider of Varania," Bob told him. "The one that's missing from the jewel vault. It has to be. It's so perfect you thought it was real, but it isn't. It's made of metal. Like the one we saw, only better."

Jupiter walked over and touched the jeweled spider. "You're right," he said. "That's a masterpiece. It just has to be the real thing. Where did you find it?"

"Under my handkerchiefs. Someone hid it there. It wasn't there this morning, I know."

Jupe's brow furrowed. He was thinking hard.

"Why would anyone hide the silver spider of Varania in our room?" he asked, mostly to himself. "It doesn't make sense, unless someone planned to accuse us of stealing it. In that case—"

"What shall we do, Jupe?" Pete asked anxiously. "Why, it's the death penalty just to be caught with that spider!"

"I think—" Jupe began. But they had no chance to find out what he thought. Down the hall outside their room came the tramp of heavy feet. There was a loud knock on the door, then someone tried the knob. An angry voice cried, "Open the door in the name of the Regent! Open for the law."

After a startled second, Jupiter and Pete flung themselves at the door and slammed into place a big iron bolt.

Bob, too surprised to think clearly, just stood with the silver spider of Varania in his hand, wondering dizzily what to do with it.

Chapter 7
Flight!

K N U C K L E S thundered commandingly on the door again.

"Open in the name of the Regent! Open for the law!" a voice shouted again.

Pete and Jupiter leaned against the door as if their weight would help keep the door shut. Bob stared at the beautifully enameled silver spider in his hand and his mind ran around in wild circles. He had to hide it. But where?

He ran around the room, looking frantically for a hiding place and seeing none. Under the carpet? No good! Under the mattress? No good either! Then where? Where would it go undiscovered?

Heavy blows thudded on the door. The guards were breaking it down. Then things became even more confusing. The curtains at the window were flung aside and a young man stepped through. Pete and Jupiter whirled to meet this new attack.

"It's me, Rudy!" the newcomer whispered loudly. "And my sister Elena!"

Elena stepped out beside him, wearing a boy's trousers and jacket.

"Come on!" she urged. "You have to flee. They're going to arrest you for high crime against the state."

The blows against the door thudded methodically. Someone was using an ax. But the door was oak, three inches thick, and it would hold for several minutes.

It was like a scene from a movie. Everything was happening too swiftly for any of the boys to react calmly. The one thing they knew was that they had to get out of there.

"Come on, Pete!" cried Jupiter. "Bob, bring the silver spider and let's go!"

Bob hesitated for a long moment, then ran to join the group. Elena led the way out onto the balcony.

They crowded together in the cool darkness, the city lights gleaming below. "The ledge goes around the side of the building to the back," said Elena. "It's wide enough if you keep your nerve. I'll lead."

She climbed over the balustrade of the balcony onto a stone ledge. Jupiter hesitated.

"My camera!" he said. "I forgot it."

"No time now!" Rudy said urgently. "The door will give us two minutes more, maybe three. We can't waste a second."

Reluctantly abandoning the camera-radio, Jupe followed Pete. Faces to the wall, they pressed themselves against the rough stone of the castle and moved after Elena, who was traveling as fast and surely as a cat.

There was no time to feel scared. Behind them they could still hear the crashing blows against the door to their room. They came to a corner. The night wind plucked at them and for a moment Bob swayed, losing his grip. Far below him ran the Denzo River, dark and swift in the night. Rudy's hand, gripping his shoulder, steadied Bob. He regained his balance and followed the others.

"Faster!" Rudy breathed in his ear.

A pair of pigeons, disturbed from their roost on the ledge, flapped wildly around their heads. Bob resisted an impulse to duck, and followed the others over a balustrade onto another balcony. Here all five gathered for a moment.

"Now we have to climb!" Elena whispered fiercely. "I hope you're good climbers because it's the only way. Here's the rope. It has knots in it. There's another rope, hanging down to the balcony below, but that's to fool them into thinking we went that way."

A rope dangled down from above. She started up it. Pete followed easily, Jupiter, grunting and puffing, more slowly. Bob gave him a chance to get up several feet, then grasped the rough knots of the dangling rope and started after him.

Rudy had left them for a moment. Daringly he went back along the ledge to peer around the corner. He called softly, "They're still getting through the door. But we've got to get out of sight."

"What?" Bob paused to listen to Rudy. As he turned his head, his right hand slipped from the knot he was holding. The rope slipped through his fingers and he was falling backwards, down into the darkness.

He crashed against something that broke his fall— Rudy—and they both went tumbling to the balcony. Bob's head hit against the stone, and waves of red and yellow light seemed to pass before his eyes.

"Bob!" Rudy bent over him. "Bob, can you hear me? Are you hurt?"

Bob opened his eyes and blinked. The waves of colored lights flickered and went away. He could see Rudy's face bending close to his. He was lying on stone, and his head hurt.

"Bob, are you all right?" Rudy asked urgently.

"My head hurts," Bob said, "but I guess I'm all right." He sat up slowly and looked around. He was on a balcony, that much he could tell. Beside him the dark bulk of the castle towered upward, below him was the river and the faraway lights of Denzo.

"What am I doing here?" he asked Rudy. "I saw you come in the window and yell to us to get out, and now I'm out on the balcony and I've got a lump on my head. What happened?"

"Prince Paul protect us!" Rudy groaned. "You fell and addled your brain. No time for talk. Can you climb? Here. This rope. Can you climb it?"

He put the rope in Bob's hand. Bob felt it. As far

as he knew he had never seen the rope before. He felt weak and wobbly. His head throbbed.

"I don't know," he said. "I'll try."

"Not good enough." Rudy made a quick estimate of his condition and came to a swift decision. "We'll pull you up. Stand still. Let me loop this rope around your chest, under your shoulders."

He tied the free end of the rope securely around Bob's chest.

"There!" he said. "Now I'm going to climb up and then we'll pull you. The wall is rough and has cracks. Maybe you can help. If not, just let yourself go limp. We won't drop you." To those above, he called: "I'm coming. Something's happened."

He swarmed up the rope into the darkness. Bob stood there fingering the lump on the back of his head and wondering how he had gotten where he was. He and the others must have followed Rudy, but he couldn't remember doing it. The very last memory he had was of seeing Rudy at the window while those axes pounded on the door of his room.

Up above, Rudy clambered through a window where the others waited anxiously.

"Bob took a tumble," he said. "He's shaken up. We have to pull him. With all four of us, we can do it. Come on now, heave."

They got what slack there was in the rope, and tensed themselves to pull. The knots in the rope proved a hindrance—each one had to be eased over the window sill. But Bob wasn't heavy and presently his head and shoulders appeared outside the window. He grabbed for a handhold and pulled himself in, shaking off the rope.

"Here I am," he said. "I'm okay, I guess. I mean my head hurts but I can move all right. I just can't remember getting onto that balcony."

"That doesn't matter," Elena spoke up. "As long as your head is clear now."

"I'm okay," Bob repeated.

They were in another bedroom of the castle. This one was damp and dusty, and had no furniture in it. Rudy and Elena tiptoed to the door, opened it a crack and peered out.

"The coast is clear for the moment," Rudy reported. "Now we have to get you to a hiding place. What do you think, Elena? Shall we lead them down to the cellars?"

"The dungeons, you mean!" Elena said. "No, I don't think so. The rope we left will cause the guards to search all the lower part of the palace. They'll expect Jupiter and Pete and Bob to try to get out that way. Look."

She stood at the window and pointed down. In the small bit of courtyard they could see below, lights were moving.

"They already have guards out in the courtyard," she said. "My idea is to go upward, to the roof. Later, tomorrow night maybe, we'll try to sneak them down into the dungeons and out through the sewers into the city. Then they can get to the American Embassy and take refuge."

"Good idea," Rudy agreed. He turned to the three. "We're going up," he said. "This part of the castle isn't in use and won't be searched if we can make them think you've gone downward. Give me your handkerchief, Jupiter."

He took from Jupiter's jacket pocket a folded white handkerchief with "J. J." monogrammed on it.

"We'll drop this for a false clue later," he said. "Now follow me. Elena, you keep watch in the rear."

He wrapped the rope around his waist, then led the way out into the hall. They moved swiftly but silently down the unlit stone hallway, then up a stairway to a still higher, pitch-dark hall.

Using his flashlight, Rudy located a door that was almost invisible in the dark wall. It opened with a loud squeaking of hinges that startled them all. But no alarm was raised; apparently no one was on these upper floors.

They slipped through like ghosts and went up a very narrow flight of stone steps. Another door led them out onto the broad roof of the castle. Stars glowed brightly in the sky overhead. A wall of stone surrounded the roof, cut at intervals with niches.

"Those were for shooting arrows, or pouring boiling oil down on attackers," Rudy said, gesturing. "Nowadays everything is peaceful so the roof isn't used for a look-out station any more. But there are still sentry huts at each corner. Over here."

He led the way across the castle roof to a small, square stone building at one corner. Its wooden door opened with some protest. Rudy's flashlight showed a dusty interior with four wooden benches that were wide enough to be beds, of a sort. There were narrow windows with no glass in them.

"Once sentries watched in shifts from each of these sentry huts," Rudy said. "But those days are long past. You should be safe here until we can come for you, probably tomorrow night."

Jupiter dropped down onto a wooden bench.

"I'm certainly glad the weather is warm," he said. "But what is this all about, anyway?"

"Some kind of plot," Elena replied. "You were to be arrested for stealing the royal silver spider of Varania, and somehow used to force Prince Djaro to give up the throne. That's as much as we know. It's all obviously nonsense, because you couldn't steal the silver spider even if you wanted to."

"No," Jupiter said slowly. "We couldn't have stolen it. But just the same, we have it. Show it to them, Bob."

Bob put his hand in his jacket pocket. Then he tried the other pocket. Becoming alarmed, he tried all his pockets. At last he swallowed hard and said, "I'm sorry, Jupe, I don't have it. In the excitement I must have lost it."

Chapter 8
Bob Can't Remember

" Y O U H A D the silver spider and you *lost* it?" Rudy stared at Bob in dismay.

"That's terrible," Elena said. "But how could such a thing happen?"

Jupiter explained how Prince Djaro had told them the silver spider was missing, and asked their help in finding it. He told of Djaro's taking them to the vault and showing them the imitation spider, and of his suspicion that Duke Stefan had removed the real one for purposes of his own—to prevent Prince Djaro's coronation. Then Bob told how he had found the real spider hidden among his handkerchiefs.

"I begin to understand the plot," Rudy muttered. "Duke Stefan had the spider hidden in your room. Then he sent men to arrest you. You were supposed to be found with the spider in your possession. Duke Stefan would claim you stole it, that Djaro by his carelessness gave you the chance. Djaro would be disgraced. You three would be expelled from the country and all ties with the United States would be broken off. Duke Stefan would continue to rule as Regent. Then, with Djaro still in disgrace, he would find some pretext for assuming the rule of Varania for himself.

"Now, though the spider is gone, he can still proceed. He will charge you with stealing it and hiding it, even if we manage to get you safely to the American Embassy."

Pete shook his head. "I still don't understand," he said, "why the silver spider is so important. I mean, suppose it had been lost in a fire or something, then what?"

"Then the whole country would go into mourning," Elena put in. "But Prince Djaro would not be blamed. Really, it's hard to explain what that silver spider of Prince Paul means to us. It's not just a jewel. It's a symbol. It represents all we treasure—our freedom, our independence, our good fortune."

"Probably we're superstitious," Rudy added. "But a legend goes with it. Prince Paul is supposed to have said, when he was crowned, that just as a spider had saved him and let him bring freedom to his people, so would freedom and fortune reign as long as the silver spider remained safe. Maybe he didn't actually say that, but every Varanian firmly believes he did. The loss of the spider would be a national calamity. To make Prince Djaro responsible for the loss, even indirectly, would make the citizens of our country, who now love him, feel he is unworthy.

"No," he finished, after a long pause, "unless we

can restore the silver spider to Prince Djaro, Duke Stefan will win."

"Golly," Bob said, gulping, "that's bad. Here, help me look again. Maybe I missed it."

This time Pete and Jupiter searched Bob's pockets, turning each one inside out. They even looked in the cuffs of his trousers. But they knew as they did so it was hopeless. Bob didn't have the spider.

"Think, Bob!" Jupiter urged. "You had it in your hand. Now what did you do with it?"

Bob frowned, trying to think.

"I don't know," he said. "The very last thing I can remember is the pounding on the door and Rudy coming in the window. Then everything is a blank until he was bending over me on that balcony."

"Partial amnesia," Jupiter said, pinching his lip. "When someone gets a blow on the head, it isn't at all unusual for him to forget what's just happened. Sometimes he forgets everything for the last few days or even weeks. Sometimes just for the last few minutes. Usually his memory for the missing time gradually comes back, but not always. That's apparently what happened to Bob. When he bumped his head on the balcony, he forgot the last three or four minutes."

"I guess that's what happened, all right," Bob sighed, feeling the bump on his head. "I have a kind of recollection of running around the room, trying to find a good hiding place for the spider. I was pretty excited, of course, but I do remember thinking it

DURING THE long night, The Three Investigators remained hidden in the sentry hut on the palace roof. No one searched that part of the castle—it was too obvious they had gone down, not up. The cleverly placed dangling rope, and Jupiter's handkerchief, which had been found at the entrance to the cellars, led the search away from the boys.

After Rudy and Elena left them, Pete, Bob and Jupiter had stretched out on the wooden benches to try to sleep. Despite the uncomfortable beds and the adventures of the evening, they slept soundly.

As the sun rose the next morning, Pete woke, yawned and stretched his muscles. Jupiter was already awake, doing some exercises to take a slight stiffness out of his muscles. Pete found his shoes, put them on and stood up. Bob was still sound asleep.

"Looks like a nice day," Pete commented, peering out the narrow slits which constituted windows in the little stone hut. "Except that it doesn't look like we're going to get any breakfast. Or lunch. Or dinner. I'd feel a lot better if I knew when we were going to eat."

"I'd feel a lot better if I knew how we were going to get out of this palace," Jupiter replied. "I wonder what Rudy's plans are."

"And I wonder whether Bob will remember what he did with the silver spider when he wakes up."

Just then Bob sat up, blinking.

"Where are we?" he asked. Then he put his hand to the back of his head. "Ouch, my head hurts. I remember now."

"You remember what you did with the silver spider?" Pete burst out.

But Bob shook his head. "I remember where we are," he said. "And I remember how my head got bumped—that is, I remember what you told me. That's all."

"No use worrying about it, Bob," Jupiter said. "We just have to wait and see if your memory comes back by itself. It may or it may not."

"Uh-oh!" Pete said, at the window. "Someone's coming out on the roof. He's looking this way!"

All three crowded to the window. A somewhat stooped man in baggy gray clothing and wearing a large apron had stepped through the doorway from the stairs. He held a broom, dustpan and cloth. He looked around stealthily, then put down his cleaning implements and came scuttling toward the sentry hut.

"Let him in, Pete," Jupiter said. "He's not a guard and he obviously knows we're here."

Pete eased the the door open and the man slipped inside. Once within, he breathed a sigh of relief.

"Wait!" he said in heavily accented English. "Make sure I was not followed."

They watched at the window for another couple of minutes. No one else appeared, and they all relaxed.

"Good," the man said. "I am a cleaner. I slipped away up the stairs. I have message from Rudy. He says does one named Bob remember?"

"Tell him no," Jupiter answered. "Bob doesn't remember."

"I will tell. Rudy says also, be patient. When it is very dark again he will come. Meanwhile, here is food."

The man reached into the pockets of his ample apron and brought out wrapped sandwiches, some fruit, and a plastic bag of water, all of which had been hidden in the capacious garment.

The boys took the food with great satisfaction. The man did not linger.

"I must hurry back," he said. "All is excitement below. Be patient and may Prince Paul extend his protection to you and to our prince."

With that he was gone. Pete gratefully bit into a sandwich.

"We'll have to ration the food to make it last all day," Jupiter remarked, passing a sandwich to Bob. "And especially the water. But it's lucky Rudy and Elena have friends in the castle."

"Lucky for us," Bob said. "What was it he was telling us last night about the organization of minstrels to assist Prince Djaro? My head hurt too much for me to listen carefully."

"Some of it you already know," Jupiter said between bites, "but I'll go over it again. Rudy said that his and Elena's father was the prime minister when Prince Djaro's father ruled. As he told us, he's a descendant of the original minstrel family that saved Prince Paul.

"When Duke Stefan became Regent, Rudy's father was forced into retirement. He suspected Duke Stefan then, and he began to organize everyone he could find who was loyal to Prince Djaro into an undercover organization to keep an eye on Stefan. They call themselves the Minstrel Party.

"Some are here in the castle as guards, or officers, and I suppose the cleaning man who brought us the food is one. Last night loyal Minstrels on the staff of guards learned of the plot to arrest us and got word to Rudy's father. By working very fast, Rudy and Elena were in time to help us. When they were children, their father lived in the palace, you remember, and they explored it from top to bottom. They know hidden passageways and tunnels and drain sewers that no one else knows about, so they can come and go unseen. Remember what Djaro told us about the palace being built on the ruins of an older castle?"

"All that is just great," Pete put in, "but we're still stuck here on top of the palace. Do you think Rudy and Elena will really be able to lead us out tonight —that is if nobody catches us before then?"

"They think so," Jupiter answered. "They plan to recruit some more Minstrels to help them, I think. We've got to get out of here so we can get that tape I gave you to the American Embassy. It's important evidence."

"I'd feel a lot better if I was James Bond," Pete grumbled. "He can get out of anything. But I'm not James Bond and neither are you. I've got a funny feeling things aren't going to go as smoothly as Rudy hopes."

"We have to do our best," Jupe told him. "Only by getting away from here can we help Djaro, and after all, that's what we came for. In any case, we can't do a thing until we hear from Rudy and Elena again. By the way, Second, did you know you finished breakfast and are already halfway through lunch?"

Pete hastily put down the sandwich he was about to bite into.

"Thanks for telling me," he said. "I'd hate to miss lunch. It looks to me as if it's going to be a long day up here on the roof."

It was indeed a long day. They took turns watching through the window slits and napping. Finally the sun set, a crimson ball behind the golden dome of St. Dominic's. The birds twittered sleepily in the parks of Denzo and went to bed.

With the coming of darkness, the palace quieted.

Soon the only people who remained awake were the guards, who sleepily manned their posts. It had been so long since anything exciting had happened in Varania that they found it hard to be alert, even though they had special orders.

Deep in the dark cellars of the castle, two figures crept noiselessly along secret routes that they alone knew. Slowly Rudy and Elena made their way upward, aided at one vital staircase by a guard who turned his back and pretended not to see them.

Presently they emerged into the night silence of the castle roof, and waited to make sure they had not been followed. Then they slipped across to the guard hut, moving so silently that they almost took Pete, who was watching, by surprise. He let them in and Rudy risked lighting a flashlight which he had covered with a handkerchief.

"We're ready to move," he told the three. "Our plan is to sneak you out of the castle and get you to the American Embassy for refuge. The rumor is that Duke Stefan has speeded up his own plans. We think that tomorrow he plans to cancel Prince Djaro's coronation and proclaim himself Regent indefinitely.

"Unfortunately we can't do anything to stop him. The people would storm the castle and rescue Prince Djaro if they knew, but there's no way to tell them he's in danger. We thought of trying to capture the radio and television station, but Duke Stefan is too cunning. He has the building heavily guarded.

"Tell me, Bob, have you remembered yet what you

did with the silver spider? It has not been found in the courtyard."

Bob shook his head. He felt terrible not being able to remember.

"If we had the spider," Jupiter asked, "would that help Prince Djaro any?"

"It might," Elena put in. "The Minstrels could issue a proclamation in the prince's name, asking the citizens of Varania for help in overcoming the tyrant, Duke Stefan. The silver spider would be a symbol that the proclamation really came from the prince. It would carry great weight—it might possibly turn the tide. Though we'd probably be arrested before we got very far."

"In any case," Jupiter said, "we ought to have the silver spider. So before we leave the castle, I propose we hunt for the silver spider along the ledges and in our room. We may yet find it where Bob dropped it."

"It will be terribly dangerous," Rudy said. "But there is the possibility we might find it. That would help. And anyway, your room is the last place anyone would expect to find you. So we'll do it."

Chapter 10
A Dangerous Descent

BEFORE THEY left the little sentry hut, they took every precaution they could think of. They picked up the paper wrappings from the food they had eaten and dropped them over the wall. The river's current would carry them away. Then they waited for the castle to settle down for the night. At last Rudy stirred.

"We have waited long enough," he said. "I have two extra flashlights here, small ones. I'll give one to you, Jupiter, and one to Pete. Use them only if you have to. I'll lead and Elena will bring up the rear. Now let's go."

In single file they crossed the roof to the door leading to the stairs. The sky was dark with heavy clouds, and big drops of rain had begun to fall.

Once inside, they went cautiously down the narrow stairs, pausing often to listen. No sounds reached them. They felt their way along, aided only by the glow of Rudy's flashlight which went on and off like a firefly.

They went down the dark corridor and then down

more stairs and along another corridor. The boys were lost, but Rudy seemed to know exactly where they were. Presently he led them into a room and bolted the door.

"Now we can rest a moment," he said. "So far so good, but this has been the easiest part. From now on there is danger. I do not think they are still looking for you in the castle, so surprise is on our side. First we must hunt for the spider. Then, whether we find it or not, we must get down to the cellars. From there we go through the dungeons and make our way to the storm sewers. We will travel through the sewers —Elena and I have already planned that part of the trip—and emerge near the American Embassy. There you will take refuge and when you are safe, the Minstrels will paste up posters all over the city proclaiming that Prince Djaro is in danger and Duke Stefan is trying to usurp the throne. After that—well, we do not know what will happen, we can only hope.

"Now we will go out the window and down to the balcony below. I have a rope around my waist. Elena has another rope, but we will save hers for an emergency."

He fastened the rope tightly and slipped out the window. When a cautious whisper told them he had reached the balcony below, Pete and Jupiter followed.

Bob and Elena peered out the window. Below them the flashlight flickered back and forth across the balcony. The boys were hunting for the silver spider, in case it had popped out of Bob's pocket when he had fallen the previous night.

At last the light went out. Rudy's whisper reached them. "Come on down."

Bob and Elena climbed down the rope, leaving it hanging so they could come back the same way.

"The spider's not here," Rudy whispered tensely as they gathered close together in the darkness. "Of course, it could have slipped through and into the river, but I don't think so. My idea is that Bob dropped it when he rushed out on the balcony outside your room."

They started edging along the ledge that ran to the corner. The lip of it was rounded, and an incautious step would send them plunging into the river that rushed below, silent and black. But they could move safely if they hugged the wall. Rudy stopped every few feet to scan the ledge with the flashlight, just on the off chance of finding the silver spider, but they reached the next balcony without discovering it.

This was the balcony outside their room. Rudy peered carefully in the window to make sure no one was in the room. Then, while the boys and Elena perched on the balcony rails, he went over every inch of the balcony with the light.

Nothing. The silver spider was not on the balcony.

"What do we do now?" Pete whispered.

"Go inside." It was Jupiter who answered. "We have to search the room."

One by one they slipped in through the window and stood in a silent row, listening. The castle seemed to be held in a deep hush. Only the sound of a cricket that had somehow found its way inside broke the quiet.

"A cricket in your room means good luck," Pete whispered. "Anyway, I hope so. We can use some."

"You said Bob was running around the room with the silver spider in his hand," Elena murmured. "He might have dropped it then. We have to search the whole room. We'll go on our hands and knees and use all the flashlights. We can't be seen from outside now."

Each took a section of the floor and on hands and knees began to cover it. Bob had no light, so he crawled beside Pete.

The light glinted on something bright. They had it!

Then, as Bob picked up the bright object, disappointment was so strong he could taste it. The bright thing was just a bit of aluminum foil from a roll of film they had opened.

After this false alarm, they continued the search. Bob even crawled under the bed, while Pete held the flashlight so he could see. A small dark creature leaped anxiously out of his way.

"Krikk!" it went. "Krikk!"

They had disturbed the cricket. Pete followed it with his light and they saw it bound from under the bed smack into the spider web which still hung in the corner of the room.

Desperately the cricket struggled to get free, but it only got entangled more tightly in the web. Two spiders were watching from the crack where the wainscoting didn't quite meet the floor. One of them ran out, skimmed over the web and began to wrap sticky threads around the cricket. In a moment it was a helpless prisoner.

Bob felt an impulse to set the cricket free, but he restrained it. That would mean destroying the spider web, and maybe killing the spider, and the spider, after all, was Varania's good-luck symbol.

"You said a cricket in the room was lucky," he muttered to Pete. "But it wasn't lucky for the cricket. I just hope the same thing doesn't happen to us."

Pete was silent. He and Bob backed out from under the bed and joined the others in front of the wardrobe, which Jupiter and Rudy were searching.

"Maybe Bob actually did hide the silver spider," Jupiter whispered. "He couldn't have dropped it or we'd have found it, if those soldiers last night didn't."

"It was not found." Rudy's voice was low. "Duke Stefan is in a rage. If it had been found he would be all smiles. So maybe Bob did hide it after all. Can you remember perhaps hiding it, Bob?"

Bob shook his head. He just couldn't remember a thing about the silver spider.

"Well, we'll look," Rudy said. "Let us examine the suitcases. Elena, you look under the mattress and the pillows—Bob might have hidden it there, not seeing any better place."

Pete and Jupiter examined the suitcases. Elena felt under the mattress, the sheets, the pillows.

The result was still nothing.

They gathered again in the middle of the room.

"It isn't here," Rudy said, his voice puzzled. "We didn't find the spider, the soldiers didn't find the spider, yet it is gone. I am afraid that when Bob ran out on the balcony, he still had it. As he climbed over the side to get to the ledge he must have dropped it. Though I still cannot think why it was not found in the courtyard."

"What shall we do now, Rudy?" Jupiter asked. Usually Jupe was the leader in anything they did, but now Rudy, being older and knowing his way about the ancient palace, was definitely in charge.

"Get you to safety," Rudy murmured. "That is all we can do. So we must go back and—"

At that moment the door burst open. Electric lights blazed on. Two men in the scarlet uniforms of palace guards rushed in.

"Stay where you are!" they shouted. "You are under arrest! We have caught the American spies!"

There was a moment of great confusion. Rudy hurled himself at the two men.

"Elena!" he shouted. "Get them to safety! Leave me!"

"Come on!" Elena cried, darting to the window. "Follow me."

Bob tried to move toward the window. As Rudy grappled with the first man, attempting to seize his legs, the second man got Jupiter by the collar. The two struggling groups fell, with Bob between them. Heavy bodies thudded down on top of him. As he fell, he hit his head again. The carpet softened the blow, but it was a solid thump.

For the second time, Bob blacked out.

Chapter 11
The Mysterious Anton

BOB LAY with his eyes closed, listening to Jupiter and Rudy talk.

"Well," Jupiter said gloomily, "here we are, caught like that cricket in the spider web. I never guessed there would be men on guard outside the door of our room."

"Neither did I," Rudy said, equally gloomy. "I thought that since it was empty they'd forget about it. Well, at least Pete and Elena got away."

"But what can they do?" Jupiter asked.

"I don't know. Maybe nothing, except tell our plight to my father and the others. It is doubtful that my father can rescue us, but he can go into hiding to avoid Duke Stefan's vengeance."

"Which leaves us and Djaro in the soup," Jupiter muttered. "We came over here to help Djaro but we certainly have been washouts."

"Washouts? I do not understand the word."

"Flops. Failures," Jupiter told him. "Look, I think

Bob is waking up. Poor Records, he's had two bad bumps."

Bob opened his eyes. He was lying on a rude cot covered with a blanket. He blinked in the dim light. Slowly his eyes focused on a flickering candle, a stone wall beside him and a stone roof above. Across the room was a solid door with only a small peephole. Jupe and Rudy were bending over him. Bob sat up, his head throbbing.

"Next time I come to Varania, I'm going to wear a football helmet," he said, and tried to smile.

"Good, then you're all right!" Rudy exclaimed.

"Bob, do you remember?" Jupe asked urgently. "Think hard now."

"Sure I remember," Bob said. "Those guards busted into the room and you and Rudy tangled with them and I got knocked down and bumped my head. I remember that much. Now I guess we're in jail someplace."

"I don't mean that," Jupiter said. "Do you remember what you did with the silver spider? Sometimes if one bump gives you amnesia, another bump will bring back your memory."

"No." Bob shook his head. "It's all still a blank."

"Perhaps it is just as well," Rudy said darkly. "Then Duke Stefan cannot force you to tell him anything."

At that moment, keys rattled outside. The heavy iron door swung inward. Two men in the uniform of the Royal Guard tramped in, shining powerful electric lanterns at them. In their right hands they carried swords.

"Come," growled one of the men. "Duke Stefan wants you in the room of questioning. On your feet. Walk between us. Try no tricks or it will be the worse for you."

He waved his sword threateningly.

The boys got slowly to their feet. With one soldier ahead of them and one behind, they tramped out into a damp stone corridor. Behind them the corridor led downward into unguessed realms of darkness. Ahead of them it sloped upward. They went past other closed doors, and up a flight of stairs. At the top of the stairs, two more guards stood at attention.

The two men hustled the boys through a doorway into a long room lit with lanterns. Bob gave a little gasp and even Jupiter turned pale. They had seen this kind of room a couple of times in horror movies. It was a torture room dating from centuries ago. And it was real.

At one side was an ugly rack where a victim was tied to have his bones stretched by heavy weights. Beyond was a huge wheel to which a victim was tied to have his arms and legs smashed by hammers. There were other devices, made of massive timbers, which they preferred not to guess about. And in the center of the room was a tall figure of a woman made of metal. The figure was just a shell, and the front was hinged so it would open. It was open now. Inside were rusty spikes sticking straight out. The idea was that someone stood inside the shell of the Iron Maiden, as it was called, and the front half was slowly closed until those rusty spikes—but neither Jupe nor Bob cared to think about that.

"The room of questioning!" Rudy whispered, and his voice trembled a little. "I've heard of it. It dates back to the reign of Black Prince John, a bloody tyrant of the Middle Ages. It hasn't been used since, that I know of. I think Duke Stefan had us brought here just to scare us. He wouldn't dare use torture on us!"

Maybe Rudy was right, but just the same, the rack, the wheel, the Iron Maiden and other devilish devices made Bob and Jupe's stomachs feel queer.

"Silence!" a guard roared at Rudy. "Duke Stefan comes!"

The guards at the door sprang to attention. Duke Stefan strode into the room, followed by Duke Rojas. On Duke Stefan's face was a look of ugly pleasure.

"So the mice are in the trap!" Duke Stefan said to the three boys. "And now it is time for them to squeal. You are going to tell me what I want to know, or it will be the worse for you."

The guards brought a chair from a corner, dusted it off, and placed it before the wooden bench where the boys were seated. Duke Stefan sat down and tapped his fingers on the chair arm.

"Ah, young Rudolph," he said to Rudy. "So you are in this. It shall go hard with your father and your family, I promise you. Not to mention yourself."

Rudy clamped his lips tightly and said nothing.

"And now you, my young Americans," Duke Stefan purred. "I have you. At least I have two of you. I will not ask you why you are here in this country. The cameras you left behind in your flight tell us everything. They prove you are agents of the American government—spies! You came here to plot against Varania. But you have committed a greater crime than that. You have stolen the silver spider of Varania."

He leaned forward, his face darkening.

"Tell me where it is," he said, "and I will be easy with you. I will assume you are just young and foolish. Come, speak!"

"We didn't steal it," Jupiter said boldly. "Someone else stole it and hid it in our room."

"So!" Duke Stefan said. "You admit you had it. That in itself is a crime. But I am tender-hearted. I feel sympathy for your youth and folly. Just tell me where it is—return it to me—and I will forgive you much."

Bob waited for Jupiter to speak. Jupe hesitated. But he could see no harm in telling the truth.

"We don't know where it is," he said. "We haven't any idea."

"You defy me, eh?" Duke Stefan scowled. "Let the other one speak. If you wish mercy, my little mouse, tell where the silver spider is."

"I don't know," Bob said. "I haven't any idea."

"But you had it!" Duke Stefan roared at them.

"That you have admitted. So you know where it is. Did you hide it? Did you give it to someone? Answer or it will be the worse for you!"

"We don't know where it went," Jupiter said. "You can ask us all night, and we won't be able to tell you anything else."

"So. You are being stubborn." Duke Stefan drummed his fingers on the arm of his chair. "We can cure that. We have instruments in this room that have made grown men, far braver than you, scream to be allowed to speak. How would you like to stand within the Iron Maiden there and have her slowly embrace you, eh?"

Jupiter gulped and was silent. Rudy spoke up boldly.

"You wouldn't dare!" he said. "You plan to take the throne from Prince Djaro, and you want the people of Varania to think you are a just and kind ruler. If it became known that you had tortured anyone, you would suffer the fate of Black Prince John long ago. Remember that the people rose and tore him limb from limb with their bare hands."

"Bold words," sneered Duke Stefan. "But I do not need the Iron Maiden nor the rack to get the truth from these culprits. I have other methods."

He signaled to the guards.

"Bring in the gypsy, Old Anton," he ordered.

"Anton the Ancient!" Rudy whispered excitedly to his friends. "He—"

"Silence!" Duke Stefan roared.

The boys craned their heads and saw an old man escorted into the room by the guards. He was tall, or would have been if he had not been bent far over as he walked, supporting himself with a stick. He wore bright-colored rags, and gold rings in his ears, and his face was drawn like a skull. Two bright blue eyes burned in his face, which was so dark that it made his eyes seem even brighter.

He shuffled forward until he stood before Duke Stefan.

"Old Anton is here," he said, his tone suggesting that he considered himself far superior to the man he was speaking to.

"I have need of your powers," said Duke Stefan. "These boys know something they will not tell. Learn it for me."

The ancient gypsy's skull-like face split in an ironic smile.

"Old Anton does not take orders," he said. "Good night, Duke Stefan."

Duke Stefan's face darkened at the impudence of the gypsy. But he restrained his anger. From his pocket he drew several gold pieces.

"I did not mean to order you, Anton," he said. "I seek your aid. I pay well. Here is gold."

The gypsy turned back. Claw-like hands reached for the gold pieces and tucked them away under the rags.

"Anton will help one who is so generous," he said, seeming to laugh at the duke. "What knowledge do you seek, Duke Stefan?"

"These young imps know where the silver spider of Varania is," Duke Stefan said. "They have hidden it but will not tell where. I could easily learn the truth with the aid of these—" he waved his hand toward the instruments of torture—"but I am merciful. Your power is great, and it is painless. Question them."

"Old Anton obeys," the gypsy cackled. He turned to the three boys. From somewhere beneath his rags he brought out a brass cup and a pouch. Into the cup he put several pinches of powdery material that looked like seeds. Then, surprisingly, he produced a modern cigar lighter and lit the powder. Thick blue smoke rose in the air.

"Breathe, small ones," Anton crooned, waving the cup back and forth in front of the three boys' faces. "Breathe deeply. Anton commands you to breathe the smoke of truth."

They tried to turn their faces aside and hold their breath, but they couldn't. The smoke got into their nostrils. They breathed it in spite of themselves. It was pungent but not disagreeable and they found themselves relaxing, their minds becoming pleasantly drowsy.

"Now look at me," Old Anton said. "Look at me, little ones, look into my eyes."

Though they wanted to resist, their heads turned. They looked into Anton's bright blue eyes and they seemed to be deep, distant pools of water into which they were falling.

"Now speak!" Anton said, his tone commanding. "The silver spider! Where is it?"

"I don't know," Rudy answered in spite of an effort to remain silent. Beside him Bob and Jupiter echoed the words. "I don't know . . . I don't know . . ."

"Ah!" Anton murmured. "Breathe again—breathe deeply."

Once more he passed the smoking cup in front of the three boys' faces. Bob felt himself drifting as if upon a very comfortable cloud high in the air.

The gypsy touched Rudy's forehead lightly with his fingers. He leaned very close and stared unblinkingly into Rudy's eyes. Rudy could not have looked away if his life depended on it.

"Now," Old Anton whispered, "do not speak. But think. Think of the silver spider. Think where it is . . . Ah!"

After a long moment he took his fingers from Rudy's forehead and repeated the same movements and words with Jupiter. Once more he said "Ah!" and came to Bob. As he touched Bob's forehead, his fingers seemed to tingle with electricity, and his eyes were all Bob could see, blue and piercing as if reading his very thoughts. Bob found himself thinking of the silver spider. Again he seemed to see it sitting in the palm of his hand. Then it vanished. He didn't have any idea where it went. He couldn't remember— there was a cloud on his thoughts . . .

The ancient gypsy seemed puzzled. He lingered

with Bob, murmuring urgently again and again, "Think! Think!" At last he sighed and turned away. Bob blinked. He felt as if released from a spell.

Old Anton bobbed his head to Duke Stefan.

"The first one," he said, "has not seen the silver spider and does not know where it is. The fat one saw the spider, but did not handle it. He doesn't know where it is. The small one had the spider in his hand and then—"

"Yes?" Duke Stefan exclaimed eagerly. "Go on!"

"A cloud comes over his thoughts. The silver spider disappears into the cloud. I have never met before such a case. He knew once where the spider went, but a blankness came into his mind and he has forgotten. Until he remembers, I can do no more."

"A thousand curses!" spat Duke Stefan. His fingers tapped the chair arm again.

"Tell me, gypsy," he began, then changed his tone. "Old Anton, I appreciate your efforts. It is not your fault that they cannot tell me where the silver spider is. But perhaps you can make a guess? You have many powers—we all know that. What of the spider? And—" he added with restrained eagerness—"what of my ambition to take the throne of Varania, so that a weak and foolish boy shall not sit upon it?"

Old Anton gave a sly smile.

"As to the silver spider, though silver, it is only a spider," he said. "As to your ambition, I hear a bell ringing victory. And now good night. Old men like me need their sleep."

Chuckling deep in his throat, he withdrew. Duke Stefan waved his hand.

"Escort him to his home," he said to the guards. Then he turned to Duke Rojas.

"You heard! The silver spider is only a spider, meaning we can ignore it, it is not important. And Anton says I shall be victorious. We know that in such matters Anton is never wrong. We wait no longer. In the morning the proclamation goes forth. Prince Djaro is under arrest and I am assuming the Regency until further notice. Denounce the United States for trying to interfere in our affairs, and proclaim the arrest of these two as spies and thieves. Offer a reward for the third. Round up all members of Rudolph's family, and all these so-called Minstrels you can find. Charge them with treason.

"By tomorrow Varania will be firmly in my grasp. After that we will decide whether to hold a public trial of these rascally boys, or merely expel them from the country. Guards! Take them back to their cell and let them meditate there."

He leaned toward Bob.

"Meanwhile, little mouse, try to remember what you did with the silver spider. Even though Anton says it is not vital, I would like to wear it around my neck when I am crowned Prince of Varania. Restore it to me and things will go easier for you.

"Now, take them away!"

Chapter 12
Into the Storm Sewers

TWO GUARDS escorted Jupiter, Bob and Rudy back to their cell in the dark underground dungeon. Rudy was in the rear and as they clattered down the flight of stone steps, the guard behind him leaned close and whispered in his ear.

"There are friendly rats in the sewers," he said.

Rudy nodded. A moment later they were ushered into the tiny stone cell with the damp stone walls and the single flickering candle. The iron door clanged shut. The two guards took up their positions outside and the boys were left alone.

They were silent for several moments, and in the silence Bob and Jupiter could hear a faint gurgling sound, as of water. Rudy explained.

"The storm sewers of Denzo pass beneath the castle," he said. "It must be raining hard outside. The rain is pouring into the drains. The storm sewers of Denzo are hundreds of years old and are not pipes, as you usually think of sewers. They are stone tunnels, sometimes taller than a man, flat on the bottom and rounded on the top. In dry weather it is possible to walk through them for miles and in wet weather one can use a small boat.

"Few people venture into them, but Elena and I and a few others know them well. If we could get into the sewers, and the water was not too deep, we could travel beneath them to safety. We could emerge into the streets near the American Embassy, and you could run there for refuge."

Jupiter pondered this information. Then he shook his head.

"We're locked in a cell," he said. "It doesn't look as if we're going anywhere."

"If we could get out of the cell for even a minute," Rudy said wistfully, "there is a manhole at the far end of the passage outside that leads into the sewers." He paused.

"There is someone there waiting to help us. One of the guards gave me a message. 'There are friendly rats in the sewers,' he said. He means some Minstrels are handy if we can get to them."

"I guess Jupe's right," Bob said. "We aren't getting out of here until Duke Stefan lets us out. Who was that gypsy, Anton? I think he read our minds!"

Rudy nodded. "At least he sensed our thoughts," he said. "Anton is the king of the few gypsies left in Varania. He is said to be a hundred years old and has strange powers no one understands. Certainly he knew the truth about the silver spider. But I am sad-

dened, for he told Duke Stefan that he heard a bell
ringing for victory. That means that our cause is hopeless. My father will be imprisoned. My friends, too.
And Elena and I . . ." He became silent.

Bob knew how he must be feeling. "We can't give
up," he said stoutly. "Even if it looks hopeless. Jupe,
do you have any ideas?"

"I have an idea," Jupiter said slowly, "about getting out of here. First we have to get the guards to
open the door. Then we have to overpower them."

"Overpower two grown men?" Rudy asked. "Without weapons? We can't do it."

"I'm remembering something," Jupiter said, frowning hard. "Of course it was just a story, but it sounded
as if it would work. It was in a book of mystery
stories Mr. Hitchcock gave us."

"What's your idea, Jupe?" asked Bob eagerly.

"In the last story," Jupiter said, "a boy and a girl
are locked up just as we are. They tear up their
sheets and weave them into ropes, and make nooses
at both ends of the ropes. Then they get their captors
to come inside the cell."

He went on to describe how the trick worked in the
story. Rudy listened with growing interest.

"It's possible!" he said in a low voice, so he
wouldn't be heard through the tiny viewing hole in
the door. "But what could we use for ropes?"

"These blankets on the cots," Jupiter said. "They're
old and the ends are ragged. We can tear them into

strips. But the strips would be strong enough so we wouldn't need to weave them. We could use strips of blanket for rope."

"It might work," Rudy muttered. "One of the guards is friendly—he would only pretend to fight us. If we got the other—all right, let's try it."

Quietly they set to work. The blankets they had been given were indeed ragged, which was fortunate as Jupiter's knife had been taken from him. They tore quite easily. Slowly, very slowly, careful to make no noise, they tore off one strip about four inches wide, then another and another.

It was slow, tiring work. In places they had to use their teeth to help the tearing along, but they kept at it doggedly. Soon they had four strips. After a time they had eight, and Jupe suggested they rest.

They stretched out on the three crude cots in the cell, but they were too impatient to rest long. Soon they were at work again. Jupiter took two of the blanket strips and tied them together tightly. Then he fashioned a big slip noose in each end. He tested it around Rudy's arms and legs, and the nooses tightened properly when pulled. Rudy was aglow with excitement and admiration.

"*Brojas!*" he whispered. "I think it will work. Will four be enough?"

"Enough for the guards," Jupe whispered back.

"Let us tear some more strips to take with us," Rudy suggested. "They will come in handy if we make it to the sewers."

They tore eight more strips and knotted them into one long rope which Rudy wrapped around his waist.

"Now for the hard part," Jupiter muttered. "Bob, stretch out on the cot and start to moan. Just a little at first, then louder. Rudy, put two of the nooses on the floor just inside the door, where anyone coming in will step in them."

When all was ready, Bob began to mutter, then groan. He groaned louder, very realistically, as if in pain. After a minute one of the guards came to the door and looked in the open peephole.

"Silence!" he ordered. "Cease the noise!"

Rudy was standing by the door, while Jupe bent over Bob anxiously, holding the candle.

"He's hurt," Rudy said in rapid Varanian to the guard. "He bumped his head when he was caught. He has a fever now. He needs a doctor."

"This is a trick, you young imps!"

"I tell you he's sick!" Rudy cried. "Come in and feel his forehead. Then take him to a doctor. If you do we'll talk. We'll tell where the silver spider is. Duke Stefan will be pleased."

Still the guard hesitated. Rudy grew more urgent.

"You know the Duke does not want these Americans really hurt," he said. "The small one needs a doctor and they are ready to give back the silver spider. Act quickly, his condition may be serious!"

"We'd better see if it's true," said the second guard, the one who had whispered the message to Rudy.

"We don't want to get in trouble with the Duke. You find out if he's really sick while I guard the door. They're just boys—we have nothing to fear."

"Very well," the first guard said. "I'll see if he has a fever. But if this is a trick they'll be sorry."

A large key squeaked in the lock. The iron door creaked open, and the guard entered the cell.

With his first step he was caught in a waiting noose. Like a flash Rudy pulled it tight and the guard fell heavily to the floor, dropping his electric lantern. Jupiter spun around and tossed another noose over the guard's head, and Rudy caught one of his waving arms in still a third noose.

"Help!" the guard bawled. "Help! The young devils have me!"

The second guard came rushing into the cell, but Rudy was waiting. A noose went around his neck. Another tightened around his leg. The nooses on the other end of the ropes were placed about the other guard, linking the two men tightly together.

As the first guard kicked and struggled, his movements tightened the nooses around the second guard, who fell on top of him. Rudy bent and whispered in his ear.

"Struggle hard! Keep struggling. Don't stop."

The guard obeyed. By struggling, both men tightened the nooses on themselves and on each other, and neither would get free. Rudy chuckled. It occurred to him that they were like two insects in a spider's web.

It was a good omen. He felt his courage and hope return.

"Quickly now!" he said. "The other guards up the corridor will hear. We must move fast. Jupiter, bring the other lantern. Follow me!"

Rudy was already moving down the corridor, toward the pitch-darkness of the lower dungeons. Bob and Jupiter raced to follow, the electric lantern making bobbing beams of light ahead of them as they ran.

They came to some stairs, ran down them, and stopped. Rudy was bent over, tugging at a big iron ring in the floor. By the light of the lantern, they saw an ancient, rusty manhole set into the stone floor.

"It's stuck!" Rudy gasped. "Rusted. I can't budge it."

"Quick!" Jupiter said. "The rope. Put it through the ring and we'll all pull."

"Yes, of course!" Rudy whirled around, spinning out of the blanket rope wound about his waist. He pulled one end through the ring. All three boys seized the rope and pulled. At first the cover wouldn't budge. Then, as they heard shouts and trampling feet behind them, they gave one tremendous heave.

The manhole cover flopped up and fell with a clang on its side, revealing a pitch-black hole from which came the sound of rushing water.

"I'll go first," Rudy gasped, pulling the rope loose. "We'll all hold on to the rope. No chance to put the cover back."

He lowered his feet into the hole, put the handle of the electric lantern between his teeth and, still holding the blanket rope, dropped from sight. Bob followed him. He didn't like the look of the hole or the sound of water underneath, but he didn't have time to hesitate.

There was an endless moment in which he was falling through nothing. Then he landed on the bed of the ancient storm sewer. It was a fall of only about six feet and he wasn't hurt, but he would have fallen into the knee-deep water if Rudy had not caught him.

"Steady!" Rudy whispered. "Here comes Jupiter. Get out of his way."

Jupiter was less lucky. Before they could grab him, he lost his balance and sat down in the flowing water. Rudy grabbed his shoulders so he did not go under completely. Puffing, Jupiter scrambled to his feet.

"It's cold!" he said.

"Just rain water," Rudy said swiftly. "We'll be wetter before we get out of here. Come on, follow me. Everybody hold on to our rope. The water is flowing toward the river, but where they meet there are heavy iron bars. We couldn't get out that way so we must go upstream."

Shouts and angry voices echoed above their heads. A lantern flashed down from above. But the boys were on the move already. Stooping, for the rounded roof of the sewer was too low for them to stand upright, they began to hurry through the swirling water.

The manhole and the voices and light receded be-

hind them. Soon their tunnel met a larger one, and
they could stand upright. They sloshed along, clutch-
ing the rope, the two electric lanterns giving out a little light but not enough to combat the total darkness
in which they moved. Bob and Jupiter heard squeaking noises and something furry, swimming, was swept
against Bob's leg. He gulped but kept walking.

"The guards will follow us!" Rudy shouted.
"They'll have to for fear of Duke Stefan. But
they don't know these sewers and I do. There's a
place up ahead where we can grab a minute's rest."

He almost pulled them along as he went. Now the
water seemed deeper. They passed a place where it
came down from above like a waterfall, thoroughly
wetting them. It must be a drain in the streets above,
Bob figured.

They waded on, through another miniature waterfall, and then abruptly came out into a large round
chamber where four tunnels intersected. Rudy
stopped and flashed his light around. They could see
a ledge around the sides of the chamber, and iron
rungs set into the rock, leading upward.

"We might get out here," Rudy said. "But we don't
dare. Too close to the palace. We'll rest on the ledge,
though. I'm sure we have several minutes before any
of the guards can catch up to us. They won't be in any
hurry to go through these sewers, you can be sure."

Thankfully they scrambled up onto the two-foot-
wide ledge which partly encircled the chamber. There
they stretched out, getting their breath.

"Golly, we did it!" Bob said finally. "Anyway, we got this far. But where are we?"

Rudy started to answer him. Then he stopped.

"Turn off the lights!" he whispered urgently.

They did so. Ahead of them in the tunnel was the faint gleam of a lantern, and it was obviously coming their way. Someone ahead of them, and the guards pursuing them from behind.

They were trapped!

Chapter 13
A Dash Through
the Darkness

" U P ! " Rudy snapped. "We have to go up to the street. I'll go first."

He began to scramble up the wet, slippery iron rungs. Bob and Jupiter followed. They had to turn one lantern on long enough to find the rungs, then they shut it off and climbed in darkness.

Rudy reached the top. Holding tight with both hands, he got his shoulders beneath one side of the iron cover and strained upward. Slowly it raised. A crack of daylight came in. He got it up another inch until he could twist his head and look out. He gave an exclamation of dismay and let the cover back down.

"A patrol of guards right on the corner, waiting!" he whispered. "By the time we got the cover off and climbed out they'd have us."

"Maybe we can hide up here," Jupiter suggested, not very hopefully.

"It's all we can do," Rudy sighed. "Let's pray they'll keep on going."

Beneath them a light glowed on the running water. Then, as they peered down, a very narrow rowboat came into view. A man sat in the rear pushing it with a pole. A girl sat in the bow, shining a powerful flashlight around.

"Rudy!" she called. "Rudy, where are you?"

"Elena!" Rudy cried. "We're up here. Stay right there."

The boat stopped. The light shone on them as the three boys scrambled down the iron rungs.

"Praise to Prince Paul!" Elena exclaimed. "We've found you. You *did* get away from them."

While the man in the rear steadied the boat, the boys scrambled in. Instantly the man turned the boat around and began sending it back the way it had come with vigorous thrusts of the pole.

"The guard gave us a message that there were friendly rats in the sewer," Rudy said to Elena.

"We've been looking for you for hours," Elena replied. "We were afraid you could never escape. Oh Rudy, I'm so glad to see you!"

"And *we're* glad to see you," Rudy said with a grin. "This is my cousin, Dmitri," he told the boys, gesturing to the man in the rear. Then he turned back to his sister. "What's happening outside?"

"No time to talk now," Elena said swiftly. "Soon, when we can stop for a minute. Look ahead!"

Ahead of them a sudden shaft of daylight cut through the darkness.

"They've lifted the manhole cover!" exclaimed

Dmitri. "They're waiting for us. We'll have to try to push through."

He gave stronger pushes on the pole. The tiny boat shot ahead, into the shaft of daylight. The boys looked up. Guards were coming down into the sewer. One of them shouted, and tried to leap into the boat to overturn it. Dmitri swerved the rear sharply and the plunging guard missed. He went splashing into the water and went under, spluttering.

In another moment they were in the darkness of the gloomy tunnel again, moving swiftly beneath the city.

"They'll follow us on foot, but they'll be slow," Rudy observed.

"More likely they'll open up the covers ahead and wait for us," Dmitri said. "Here's a junction. I'm changing course."

They had come to another large chamber where three great tunnels discharged their water. Dmitri swung the boat into the left tunnel, which was smaller than the others. Rudy seized a shorter pole, and expertly kept the bow from nudging into the stone sides. Sometimes they all had to duck their heads to get under a low spot.

"You saw Dmitri yesterday leading the band in the park," Rudy told the other two boys. "He's one of the few who know these drains as well as Elena and I."

In places, the stone ceiling dipped so close to the rushing water that Bob worried they wouldn't be able to pass. But each time they made it, and there was no sign of pursuit behind.

"Where's Pete?" Jupiter asked Elena, who crouched silently beside him.

"Waiting for us," she answered. "The boat wasn't big enough to bring him. Besides, he's better off where he is. I wanted him to get to safety, but he wouldn't until he had found you or given up hope of rescuing you."

That sounded like Pete, all right.

"Where are we now, Dmitri?" Rudy called. "I'm afraid I'm lost."

"We are making a circle to reach the hiding place," Dmitri replied. "We'll be there in five minutes."

They came to another chamber where several of the drain tunnels met. This time Dmitri selected the one in the center and pushed forward. This tunnel was larger. They could sit upright now. They continued on until suddenly they saw a pinpoint of light ahead.

"Someone's ahead of us!" Bob said in alarm.

"If we're lucky it is Pete," Elena said. "That's the meeting place."

The light grew brighter and they could see it came from an electric lantern. The lantern had been placed in a big hollow, almost like a shallow cave, in the side of the storm sewer. Pete was crouched beside it and he welcomed them enthusiastically.

"Am I glad to see you!" he exclaimed. "I was getting lonely here. Some rats wanted to keep me company but I chased them off."

Dmitri steered the boat close to the side, and Rudy wedged a rope between two rocks to hold it. Then they clambered out into the cavelike hollow. The raggedness of natural rock here contrasted with the smoothly fitted stones out of which artisans many centuries before had built the city's storm drains.

"The builders found this natural underground cave when they built the drains," Rudy explained as they flopped down on the rock to rest. "It was easier to leave it than to wall it off. I discovered it years ago. We had a secret society that explored these drains, even though our father did his best to stop us. We never realized how useful our childish games were going to be."

"Now we must take council," Elena said, looking worried. "I don't think our original plans will work."

"First tell me what has happened," Rudy requested. "Dmitri, how do you come to be here?"

"I was at your father's house when the guards came to arrest him," Dmitri said. "I escaped through the secret door. I lingered and listened. The captain taunted your father, saying, 'Your traitor son has been captured and soon you will all stand trial.' But he said nothing about Elena. I hoped she had escaped.

"I knew your plans, so I entered the storm sewers to see if I could meet Elena and help her. It was raining, the drains were running water, so I took the old boat we kept hidden."

"Yes, and Dmitri did find us, just in time," Elena

said. "Pete and I escaped from the palace the way we
had planned, and came down here. We met Dmitri
and decided to stay on watch as long as we could, just
in case you escaped. We figured your only chance
would be down from the dungeons. Well—here we
are. Now we must talk about the future."

"First let us listen to the radio," Dmitri said. "Pete,
you have it."

"Oh, yes." Pete pulled a tiny transistor radio out
of his pocket. "I turned it off because I couldn't understand what they were saying."

Dmitri snapped it on. A stream of words poured
out, in Varanian, followed by a band playing military
music. Elena translated for The Three Investigators.

"It said for all citizens of Varania to stay by their
radios and television sets for an important announcement at 8 o'clock this morning. It said the announcement is of supreme importance. It was the Prime Minister's voice—recorded, of course.

"That means that at 8 o'clock they are going to an-
nounce that a foreign plot has been uncovered—that
is you three—and that Prince Djaro is implicated and
that Duke Stefan is remaining Regent until further notice. Of course, they didn't expect you to escape—
they expected to be able to hold a public trial and
show those cameras and everything and then expel
you from the country and put Rudy and Father in
jail and, oh, everything unpleasant they can think of."

"Gosh," Bob said in dismay. "We've just made it
worse for Djaro by coming here. It would have been

better if we'd stayed home."

"No one could foresee that," Elena said. "Now we must get you to safety at the American Embassy. Right, Dmitri?"

"Correct, Elena."

"But what about yourselves? And your father? And Djaro?" Jupiter asked.

"That is for later," Elena said and sighed. "I'm afraid their plans are too well prepared for us. If we could rescue Djaro—if we could arouse the people of Denzo to his danger—we could foil the plot. But as we have already said, Duke Stefan and his gang have everything in their favor."

"Yes," Dmitri agreed, "we must get you three to safety, then see what we can do about ourselves. Our cause is lost, I'm afraid. But perhaps there will come another day. Now let us start. It is already daylight outside. In an hour the radio and television will be broadcasting the Prime Minister's announcement. By then we hope you will be safe in the American Embassy.

"So follow me. From here we go on foot. The boat will not take us all."

He dropped down into the rushing water below. One by one the others followed, holding on to the blanket-strip rope. With heavy hearts the little group made its way again through the storm sewers of Denzo.

Chapter 14
Jupiter Has
an Inspiration

IN THE CITY above them the rain had stopped, and the water in the drains became shallower. Soon it was only to their ankles and they could move freely. They passed more chambers where several dark tunnels met, but Dmitri seemed to know his way.

"We will emerge in the block where the American Embassy is located," Dmitri called back once. "Pray to heaven they do not have it guarded."

They walked for what seemed a long time, though time was hard to tell in the tunneled darkness. Certainly they covered eight or ten blocks. They came to another round chamber which marked a manhole above, and abruptly Dmitri stopped.

"What is it?" Rudy called. "We have two blocks yet to go."

"Something tells me they will surely have the spot we are heading for guarded," Dmitri said. "They will guess that is where we would go, and nab us like mice coming out of their hole. If I am correct, we are now under the flower market, behind the Church of St.

Dominic. They won't be looking for us here. We can slip up to the American Embassy from the rear."

"I believe you are right," Rudy agreed. "All right, we can't stay down here the rest of our lives. Let's go up."

Iron rungs in the rocks led upward. Dmitri reached the top, put his shoulder beneath the manhole cover and heaved.

The iron cover lifted, and clanged to the cobbled street. Dmitri scrambled out.

"Come up quickly!" he cried. "I'll give you a hand."

Dmitri's strong hand pulled Elena up, then Bob. Bob blinked in the unaccustomed daylight. It was a cloudy day, the streets glistening with the night's rain. They were in a narrow alley with old houses rising on each side. Many stalls lined the alley, and vendors in quaint costumes were arranging bright flowers and fruit for the hoped-for business of the day. They looked with amazement as the rest of the bedraggled little party came scurrying up out of the drains.

Rudy and Dmitri shoved the manhole cover back into place. Then Dmitri started down the alley, ignoring the curious looks from the flower vendors. They had covered about fifty yards when he stopped abruptly. Ahead of them two palace guards in scarlet livery had turned the corner.

"Back!" Dmitri snapped. "Hide!"

But it was too late. They had been seen. Their wet clothing was clue enough to who they were, if any was needed. The guards raised a shout and started on the run for the little band of fugitives.

"Surrender!" they bawled. "In the name of the Regent, you're under arrest."

"You have to catch us first!" Dmitri shouted defiantly. He wheeled and made a sweeping motion with his arm. "Follow me!" he exclaimed. "We'll make for the church. There's a possibility—"

The rest was lost. Already they were running after him, dodging around the people who got in their way. Behind them about a dozen guards pursued, but they were having a harder time getting through the curious flower vendors who had surged into the center of the narrow street.

"One side! One side!" the guards roared.

Above the rooftops of the ancient houses Bob could see the golden dome of St. Dominic's. He was beginning to pant with exertion. What good would it do them to hide in the church, he wondered? It would just delay their being caught. But Dmitri seemed to have a plan in mind, and this was no time to ask questions.

Behind them one of the pursuing guards slipped and fell. Several of his companions stumbled over him and they made a pile in the street, helping the fugitives gain fifty yards. Bob wondered if the guard who had fallen had really had an accident. Perhaps he was a friend who was trying to help them.

They ducked around a corner and there, a block ahead of them, loomed the stately church. And there, also a block ahead of them, were more palace guards looking their way.

They could never make the door to the church!

But apparently Dmitri was not heading for the main entrance. He swerved across the street to a small side door at the rear of the cathedral. They dashed inside, and bolted the door just as their leading pursuers reached it. Angry fists began to pound on the stout wood.

Inside the church, Bob only had time for a fleeting impression of a large, square room that did not seem to have any ceiling. It went up and up as far as he could see. On one side was a flight of stairs closed in by heavy iron grillwork. Eight thick ropes hung down from above, their ends looped through iron rings set into the stone walls.

Bob had no time to see more.

"Now we make for the catacombs," Dmitri was saying. "Do you lads know what catacombs are? They are burial regions concealed beneath the church. In ancient times people were buried there, and there are many levels, many corridors. We can hide there—"

"What's the use of hiding any more?" Jupiter spoke up unexpectedly. "They'll only catch us sooner or later."

They all stared at him.

"You're thinking something, Jupe!" Pete said tensely. "I can tell. What is it?"

"These ropes." Jupe pointed. "Do they ring the bell of Prince Paul?"

"The bell of Prince Paul?" Rudy scowled, trying to fathom what Jupiter was leading up to. "No, these are the regular church bells. The bell of Prince Paul is in the other bell tower, across the church. It hangs all by itself, and rings only on state occasions."

"Yes." Jupiter spoke swiftly. "But Prince Djaro told us also that hundreds of years ago, when Prince Paul quelled the rebellion, he summoned his loyal followers to let them know he was not dead by ringing the bell."

They all stared at him. Dmitri rubbed his jaw.

"Yes," he said. "Every schoolchild knows the story. It is part of our national heritage. But what are you thinking?"

"He means that if we ring the bell of Prince Paul now, maybe the people will rise to Prince Djaro's aid!" Rudy cried. "We never thought of it—to us it is just an old story that happened long ago. All we could think of was newspapers, or the radio, or television. But just suppose if, today—"

"The bell started ringing!" Elena chimed in, tremendously excited. "And after all those radio announcements of an important message to come. The people love Prince Djaro. If they thought he was in trouble and needed them, they'd flock to his aid."

"But if—" Dmitri began.

"There's no time for ifs!" Rudy cried. "Listen to them hammer on that door. We only have moments."

"Very well." Dmitri no longer hesitated. By now guards were probably racing around to the main entrance also. "Rudy, you lead them. Elena and I will go the other way. Down to the catacombs. If they follow us, you'll gain time. Elena, we need something for them to find. Give me one of your shoes."

Elena stooped and wrenched off a wet shoe. She handed it to him.

"I'll leave it behind like Cinderella," she said, and even managed a smile. "Go, Rudy, hurry!"

"This way!" Rudy said. "Follow me!"

He ran across the cathedral to the bell tower on the other side. Bob, Pete and Jupiter followed him. Elena and Dmitri hurried toward a rear door, which presumably led to the catacombs.

Bob found himself falling behind. He was limping now. His leg, which until recently had worn a brace to strengthen it following a bad break, was beginning to pain him after so much exertion.

Ahead of him he saw the others stop. Limping more with each step, he caught up with them and saw that they were in another room similar to the one they had left. This, too, had no ceiling. A single sturdy rope hung down from above and was secured to the wall. Stairs, enclosed like the others in iron grillwork, led upward.

Rudy swiftly undid the bell rope so it hung free. Then he ran for the stairs.

"Come!" he called. "Up! Swiftly!"

Pete grabbed Bob's arm to help him, and they began to scramble frantically up the stone steps.

Chapter 15
The Bell of Prince Paul

THE STONE STAIRS were steep. For Bob each one was an effort. Rudy saw his difficulty and stopped. He handed one end of the blanket rope to Bob.

"Hang on!" he cried. "I'll give you some help."

Grasping the rope as Rudy pulled, Bob found the going easier. They went up one flight, two. As yet the guards had not found their trail. At the top of the third flight they came to a massive gate closing off the stairs. It opened with a creaking protest when pushed.

When they were through, Rudy put into place an enormous iron bolt.

"That's to hold off pursuers," he said. "In the old days, even the church might be invaded by soldiers. The priests could retreat to the bell towers, locking these gates behind them. There are two more."

They had just locked the second gate when the guards came pouring into the base of the bell tower. They looked up, saw the fugitives, and began to race up the stairs. But the first locked gate stopped them.

They shook it without effect, and bawled orders for tools to cut through the iron bars.

"They won't get through in a hurry," Jupiter puffed, as they hurried on. "We'll have a little time, anyway."

Now they were above the dome of St. Dominic's. They could see miniature people and tiny cars moving on the streets below. Everything was normal, it seemed. Except here, in the bell tower. Here was warfare and an enemy they had to outwit.

They reached the open bell-chamber, where the great bell of Prince Paul hung from massive timbers beneath a pointed roof. Here was the third gate. They slammed it shut and Rudy bolted it. A flock of pigeons, frightened by the noise, flapped away from their roosts on the ledges of the tower.

The boys paused to get their breath. Down below, the guards were attacking the first bolted gate with a great deal of noise and confusion, but no apparent progress.

"They'll send for an expert soon," Rudy guessed. "We'd better get started. Now let's see, how can we make this bell ring? Oh, first of all we'd better pull up the bell rope. They might think to fasten it down below."

In the floor of the bell-chamber was a large hole for the bell rope. Standing beneath the great bell, Rudy grasped the rope and started to pull. With Pete and Jupiter helping, they brought it up in great coils like a fuzzy snake. The guards below let out a yell as they saw the rope go up, but they were too late to catch the dangling end.

The rope safely up, the boys studied the bell. It was impressive in size, with a Latin inscription around the lip. The bell rope ran over a wheel on one side of the bell. By turning the wheel, the bell itself swung to hit the heavy clapper. This puzzled the boys, who had only seen small bells that were rung by making the clapper swing.

"Golly," Pete said as he surveyed the size of the bell. "How can we ever ring *that?*"

"We can't do it the regular way from up here," Jupiter said thoughtfully. "We'll have to tilt the bell on its side. Then we can pull on the clapper and make it hit the bell. I think that will work."

All four boys took hold of the bell rope. At Jupiter's signal, they pulled. Slowly the wheel turned and the heavy bell tipped until it was hanging on its side, the clapper just a few inches from the metal.

Rudy took the bell rope and wound it around one of the bell-chamber's ornate pillars. He fastened the rope so it held the bell in its unusual position, and they rested for a moment.

The sun was coming out and a fresh breeze blew through the open bell-chamber. Pigeons fluttered around, landing on ledges and then flying off again with loud cries.

"What time is it?" Jupiter asked, and Rudy looked at his watch.

"Twenty minutes to eight," he said. "Twenty minutes before the Prime Minister makes his speech on radio and television. We have to hurry."

"Lucky we still have the blanket rope," Jupiter said thoughtfully. "We have to get it around the clapper and then swing the clapper so it hits the bell."

It was the work of only a minute to loop the blanket rope around the pear-shaped clapper. When it was firmly in place, Rudy and Pete, as the strongest, stood back a little and gave a pull. The clapper swung. It hit the bell.

The deep, sonorous clang almost deafened the boys. Bob, peering down, saw people below turn and look up in curiosity.

"This is going to be hard on our ears!" Jupiter exclaimed. "I wish we had some cotton to put in them. Bob, Pete, do you have handkerchiefs?"

They dug them out of their pockets and rapidly tore them into small squares. They rolled the cotton squares into balls and stuffed one into each ear. Then they set to work with a will to make the legendary bell of Prince Paul ring.

Pete and Rudy did most of the work. Pulling the clapper back and letting it swing, they got a series of deep notes much faster than if the bell had been rung in the usual way. After a minute they paused, then the great bell boomed again, so loud that it seemed it must be heard all over the kingdom of Varania. The very irregularity of the bell cried *Alarm! Alarm!*

They could no longer hear the guards below. Their ears were deafened by the bell in spite of the cotton

wadding. But Bob crouched at one of the openings in the bell-chamber and peered down.

A crowd was gathering in the streets. Moment by moment more people came running, looking toward the tower where the great bell rang its solemn message of warning. Would they get the idea that Prince Djaro was in danger and needed help?

Jupiter came and crouched beside Bob. He pointed. There was a disturbance in the crowd. Several men seemed to be shouting and pointing toward the distant palace. There was a stir in the mass of people. Like a stream it began to flow away, toward the palace.

Palace guards, visible in their red uniforms, were attempting to fight their way into the crowd, but they were pushed aside. The crowd grew, and even as it did, more and more people moved toward the palace.

It looked as if the message for help was getting across!

Abruptly the bell ceased to ring. Pete and Rudy had come to look down. Rudy had his transistor radio in his hand. It was turned on, but they could hear nothing. Then the boys remembered the cotton wadding in their ears and pulled out the plugs.

A shrill voice was shouting on the radio. Rudy translated.

"It's the Prime Minister. He is saying that a grave plot against Varania has been uncovered. The coronation is postponed indefinitely. Duke Stefan is taking command of the nation and will bring the criminals—that means you—to justice. Prince Djaro is in protective custody. He appeals to all Varanians to help him uphold law and order."

"Golly, that sounds bad!" Pete said. "It sounds so believable, somehow, when it's all a lie."

"But nobody is listening to it!" Rudy cried in glee. "Everybody in the city has heard the bell and is out in the streets to find out what it means. Look at the crowds. And many of them are going toward the palace. I wish we could see what is happening there."

"Look!" Jupiter exclaimed. "The guards have broken through the gates. They're coming up!"

They all turned toward the stairs. Scarlet-uniformed guards were indeed racing up the stairs. They reached the last gate, just outside the bell-chamber, and rattled it menacingly.

"Open in the name of the Regent!" an officer shouted. "You're all under arrest!"

"Then arrest us!" Rudy cried defiantly. "Come on, Pete, we can ring the bell until they get through."

He and Pete seized the rope again and began to swing the heavy clapper. Again the bell sounded its wild cry of alarm over the city, seeming to urge every Varanian to action. A few feet away the guards were using sledge hammers and crowbars on the gate.

For five more minutes the boys made the bell of Prince Paul ring its appeal to Varania. Then with a clang the gate went down and the guards swept in and overpowered them.

"Now," the furious officer in charge bawled at them, "you're going to get what you deserve!"

Chapter 16
On the Trail
of the Spider

T H E   B O Y S did not resist as they were hustled down the long flight of stairs. At the bottom more guards formed a tight ring around them and hurried the boys out the side entrance of the church. There were still people in the streets, but not as many now. They stared curiously, and moved away only when the guards shouted at them.

The guards marched the boys along a couple of blocks to an old stone building. Inside, two officers in blue police uniforms greeted them.

"Criminals against the state!" the guard officer snapped out. "Put them in cells until Duke Stefan sends orders as to their fate."

The police hesitated.

"The bell of Prince Paul—" one said.

"Regent's orders!" the guard barked. "Move."

The police officer gave in. He led the way down a hall to where four iron-barred cells stood empty. Pete and Rudy were thrust into one, and Jupe and Bob into another facing it. The cell doors clanged shut.

"Guard them carefully or you will suffer for it!" cried the guard. "Now we must get back to the palace to inform the Regent."

They were left alone. Rudy sank down on one of the two cots in his cell. "Well, they've got us now," he called wearily. "We did our best. I wonder what is happening at the palace."

Jupiter sat down on his cot. "We've been up all night," he said. "I guess the only thing we can do is rest while we wait. However, the bell as an alarm signal—"

What he was going to say was lost in a great yawn. He rubbed his eyes. Then he looked. Bob was fast asleep. Across the corridor Pete and Rudy weren't listening. They were asleep, too. When Jupiter started to say something, however, he liked to finish it. So he continued, even though no one was listening.

"The bell as an alarm signal is hundreds of years old," he muttered, falling back on the cot. "Much older than radio or television. In Constantinople, after the Turks captured it in 1453, the use of bells was strictly forbidden lest they should provide a signal to the people for revolt and—and—"

For once he did not finish. He was asleep, too.

Bob had lost his footing in the dark, rushing waters of the drains beneath Denzo. He was being swept along, jostled and bumped against the sides, while Jupiter shouted at him from far away, "Bob, Bob!"

Bob struggled to stand up. Somebody grabbed his

arms. Jupiter's voice shouted in his ear. "Bob! Wake up! Wake up!"

Bob blinked sleepily, and yawned. With an effort he sat up. Jupe, looking a bit sleepy himself, was grinning at him.

"Bob! We have a visitor. Look who it is."

Jupe stepped aside and Bob saw Bert Young smiling at him.

"Good work, Bob!" Bert exclaimed, stepping forward and giving his hand an enormous squeeze. "All of you, it was terrific! We were worried and I do mean worried when you stopped contacting us. But it looks as if you accounted for yourselves far better than we ever figured you could."

Bob blinked at him. Then he asked, "Prince Djaro? Is he safe?"

"Couldn't be finer. He's on his way here now," Bert Young said. "Duke Stefan and the Prime Minister and all the guards who were in their private pay are under arrest. Rudy's father has just been released from jail and appointed prime minister again. But I'm sure you want to know what happened after you started ringing that bell like crazy, don't you?"

They did. Rudy and Pete crowded into the cell while the police officers stood outside, smiling at them. There wasn't a palace guard officer in sight.

Bert Young made his story as brief as he could. That morning—it was now after noon—he and the United States Ambassador had gone to the palace to try to find out what had become of Pete, Jupiter and

Bob. The gates had been locked and palace guards refused them entrance.

They were still arguing with the guards when the bell of Prince Paul began its ominous ringing. The first sounds had struck everyone dumb with surprise. Then, as the ringing continued, people began to gather in the street outside the palace gates.

The crowd grew and grew until the square opposite the palace was jammed with people. Men began shouting for Prince Djaro. The guards were helpless to drive them away. Then someone climbed high on a gate post and shouted to the crowd that Prince Djaro must be in danger, that the bell could mean nothing else, and that they must rescue him.

"Then I got into the act." Bert Young grinned. "I know some Varanian so I started shouting, too. 'Save Prince Djaro! Down with Duke Stefan!' Things like that. By now the crowd was pretty worked up and they surged against those gates and broke them open with a terrific snap. People poured in and I was with them. I made contact with the man who first started shouting, and he told me he was a Minstrel.

"We led the way into the palace. That mob just swept the guards aside as if they were matchsticks. My companion, Lonzo—"

"That's my brother!" Rudy interjected proudly. "So he escaped, too!"

"Yes. And he knew the way to Prince Djaro's apartments. We led the mob that way and when the guards saw what was happening, they changed sides pretty quick. Most of them didn't give any more trouble. We got Djaro free, and he took charge like a real prince. He ordered the guards to arrest Duke Stefan and the Prime Minister. Those rascals tried to hide, but they were caught.

"It took some time to run down all of the disloyal guards, but the rest, who were always secretly loyal to the prince, did it. Prince Djaro is busy making sure all the plotters are arrested, but he'll be here as soon as he can. By the way, it seems that your near-collision with Djaro's car in California was no accident either. It was part of the plot to get rid of the prince."

A shout in the corridor interrupted him.

"The Prince!" the cry went up. "Long live the Prince!"

Then Djaro himself appeared. He was pale, but his eyes glowed. He entered the cell, and they all squeezed back to make room for him.

"My American friends!" he exclaimed, and embraced each of them. "You saved the day. Ringing the bell of Prince Paul was an inspiration. How did you come to think of it?"

"Jupiter did it," Rudy spoke up. "We were so busy thinking of radio and television and newspapers as the only way to get a message to the people, we never thought of the bell."

"You told us," Jupiter said to Djaro, "that your ancestor Prince Paul used the bell to summon aid in the revolution of 1675. Since then the bell has only been used on royal occasions. But I thought that this was the time to use it for an alarm again.

"After all, bells are centuries older than radio and television, and even newspapers. They've always been used to summon people, to signal curfew, to warn of danger, and so on. Therefore—"

Again he was unable to finish. Djaro laughed happily and clapped him on the back.

"You did splendidly!" he cried. "Prince Paul himself would have been proud of you. Duke Stefan is in jail under guard and the plot—which I learned was far graver than I ever realized—is smashed. I have ordered the bell of Prince Paul to ring until nightfall as a signal of victory. So all is well, even though the silver spider of Varania is still lost."

"A bell rings for victory," Jupiter muttered, and for a moment his jaw dropped. Then he snapped to attention.

"Prince Djaro," he said, "I think I have deduced where the silver spider is. But to find it we have to go to the palace."

Fifteen minutes later they were riding in Prince Djaro's car through cheering crowds that blocked the streets. Prince Djaro had to bow and wave constantly, as the car inched along. But at last they reached the palace, and the bedroom that had been assigned to The Three Investigators. Pete, Jupiter, Bob, and Prince Djaro went inside.

"Now," Jupiter said, "to test my deduction. I'm

almost sure it is correct, because everywhere else has been searched. There is only one place the spider could be. I may be wrong, but—"

"Less talk and more action!" Pete groaned. "This is no time to make a speech. Show us!"

"All right." Jupiter turned toward the corner of the room. He got down on his hands and knees and crawled slowly toward the big spider web that still hung from the bed to the wall.

A large black and gold spider scuttled away from him and disappeared in the crack between the floor and the wainscoting. Another black and gold spider watched Jupiter from the crack with beady eyes.

Jupiter stretched out his hand carefully. He slid it under the web, breaking only a few strands. They all expected the second spider to retreat, but it didn't. Jupiter caught it with the tip of his finger and edged it out from the crack. He pulled it beneath the web, stood up, and extended his palm to Djaro.

"Look!" he said.

"The silver spider of Varania!" Prince Djaro cried, taking it. "You found it!"

"I finally deduced where it was," Jupiter told him. "You see, just as the guards were hammering on the door and Rudy was urging us to flee, Bob had a brilliant inspiration."

"I did?" Bob asked doubtfully. He wished he could remember having it.

"Yes, except that you forgot all about it when you bumped your head on the balcony. You realized that the one place people wouldn't expect to find an artificial spider was near a real spider web. So you slid the silver spider into the crack behind the web. We all saw it when we were searching the room and none of us thought a thing about it. Though I should have realized two spiders don't share the same web."

"*Brojas,* Bob! Well done!" exclaimed Djaro, clapping him on the back. "I knew I could count on you, my American friends."

Jupiter continued. "It was only when you, Prince Djaro, mentioned the bell ringing for victory that it came to me. Last night Old Anton, the gypsy king, made a very strange remark. He told Duke Stefan he heard a bell ringing for victory, and that the spider, though silver, was only a spider.

"I don't know what Old Anton's powers are, but somehow he knew more than he told. The bell ringing for victory, of course, turned out to be ringing for you. And I realized that if a spider was only a spider, we should look for it where we'd look for any other spider—near a spider web."

It was a long speech, but this time no one stopped him. When he had finished, he took a deep breath.

"So you see," he finished, "I don't deserve much credit. In fact—"

"You deserve all the credit I can give you!" Djaro cried delightedly. He carefully wrapped the silver spider of Varania in his handkerchief and put it in his pocket. "I can't show my appreciation fully, but I'll do the best I can right here and now."

From his other pocket he pulled out three beautifully wrought spiders of plain silver, on silver chains.

"Stand in a row, please," he directed The Three Investigators, and when they did, he hung a silver spider around each one's neck.

"Now," he grinned, "you are all three members of the Order of the Silver Spider. It is the highest decoration in my power, and given only to those who do something exceptional for Varania. It can only be worn by Varanians, so I hereby proclaim that all three of you are honorary citizens of my country. Now, what more can I do to show my gratitude? Ask me anything in my power."

"Well—" Jupe began.

But it was Pete who spoke for them. "Could we have something to eat?" he asked.

A FINAL WORD
FROM ALFRED HITCHCOCK

THERE IS but little more to add to the story of The
Three Investigators and the silver spider of Varania.
To the enthusiastic acclaim of all Varania, Prince
Djaro was crowned and took over the guidance of his
country immediately, without waiting for the elabo-
rate ceremonies that had been planned. Duke Stefan
and his cohorts were jailed, and the foreigners who
were plotting to turn Varania into a crooks' kingdom
were captured trying to escape, and given long jail
sentences.

Our three boys' part in the overthrow of the sinister
plot was not made public for reasons of national pol-
icy. However, Jupiter, Pete and Bob were interested
spectators at the coronation, and then hurried back
home. They took with them Prince Djaro's warmest
thanks and an invitation to return sometime for a
longer visit, which they hope to do.

To their regret they weren't able to keep their special camera-radios, but they were proud to bring back
the decorations they were given by Prince Djaro—the
Order of the Silver Spider. Since then they have had

an entirely new attitude toward spiders, most of which are humble and hard-working creatures who help keep down the insect population.

The Three Investigators are now scanning their mail for leads to new and interesting mysteries. I'm sure one will soon come their way, though for the life of me I can't imagine what adventure they will get into next. The only thing I'm sure of is that it will be exciting.

ALFRED HITCHCOCK